Nature
Girl

Nature Girl

a guide to caring for God's creation

Rebecca White
and Karen Whiting

ZONDERKIDZ

Nature Girl

Copyright © 2014 by Karen Whiting and Rebecca White

This title is also available as a Zondervan ebook.
Visit www.zondervan.com/ebooks

Requests for information should be addressed to:
Zonderkidz, 3900 Sparks Drive, Grand Rapids, Michigan 49546

Library of Congress Cataloging-in-Publication Data

White, Rebecca, 1976-
        Nature girl : a guide to caring for God's creation / by Rebecca White And
   Karen Whiting.
           pages cm
        ISBN 978-0-310-72500-8 (softcover)
           1. Human ecology--Religious aspects--Christianity--Juvenile literature. 2.
   Conservation of natural resources--Citizen participation--United States--Juvenile
   literature. 3. Girls--Religious life--Juvenile literature. I. Whiting, Karen H. II. Title.
   BT695.5.W55 2014
   261.8'8--dc23   2013036905

Editor: Kim Childress
Cover illustration: Jennifer Zivoin
Cover design: Deborah Washburn
Interior design: Ben Fetterley and Greg Johnson
Interior composition: Greg Johnson/Textbook Perfect

Printed in the United States of America

14 15 16 17 18 19 20 21 /DCI/ 20 19 18 17 16 15 14 13 12 11 10 9 8 7 6 5 4 3 2 1

To our girls
Elizabeth Pena
Lily Whiting
Lydia Pena
Julia Pena

Contents

Introduction

You don't have to move into the woods and live off the land to go green. Going green is about making God's earth a healthy place to live—whether you're a country gal, city dweller, or suburbanite! It's really just about making smart choices. Start with little actions, such as picking up one piece of trash a day while you're walking to school or to your BFF's house. Just think, if you plus five of your friends each pick up one piece of litter daily, that equals more than two-thousand (yep, that's 2,000!) pieces of litter a year.

Going green is also about enjoying nature and discovering more about the earth. It's about showing respect and appreciation for the beautiful planet God created for us. This book is chockfull of fun activities—experiments, crafts, recipes, games, challenges—to get you more tuned in to the goodness of God's earth. So roll up your sleeves, sister, and get ready to have some earth-friendly fun! You're going to discover so much more about God by *reeeeaaally* checking out the world he made ...

"*Ever since the world was created it has been possible
to see the qualities of God that are not seen. I'm talking
about his eternal power and about the fact that he is God.
Those things can be seen in what he has made.*"

ROMANS 1:20, NIrV

To me, going green means to help the environment.

— SKYLAR, AGE 10, FLORIDA

Green List:
The ABC's of Going Green

Here's an A-to-Z list of ideas for going green, complete
with leads to chapters about related topics. There's no
need to read this book in order—unless, or course,
you feel like it. Otherwise, open up a page and jump
right in …

Adopt a piece of earth to clean, plant, and water
when needed (Chapter 3)

Build a bird feeder, such as a peanut on a string, or a
fancy wooden feeder (Chapter 4)

Compost vegetable and grain leftovers to make
mulch (Chapter 3)

Detect water leaking from faucets, pipes, and toilets
(Chapter 5)

Explore a waterway, such as a river, lake, or ocean, for
critters and sea creatures (Chapter 5)

Form a neighborhood litter patrol to pick up litter
weekly (Chapters 9, 10)

Go local by buying stuff produced nearby, which saves gasoline (Chapter 2)

Help teach others what you learn about going green and saving energy (Chapter 10)

Investigate insects and how they help the earth (Chapter 4)

Journal about nature and what you're doing to care for the earth (Chapter 10)

Keep on keepin' on when it comes down to conserving energy (Chapter 7)

Look for animal tracks, and figure out which creatures made them (Chapter 4)

Mulch plants and trees (Chapters 3, 6)

Nurture a pet with food, water, grooming, and lots of attention (Chapter 4)

Observe a bird or animal and photograph it (Chapters 4, 10)

Plant trees and flowers (Chapters 3, 9)

Quiet yourself, sit outside, and listen to the sounds of nature (Chapter 1)

Recycle everything you can (Chapter 8)

Sow seeds in the yard or a window garden to add oxygen to the air (Chapter 6)

Treasure what God made by enjoying nature and praising God for all he created (Chapter 10)

Use less stuff, period (Chapter 8)

Visit an animal shelter and volunteer to help (Chapter 4)

Walk or bike instead of riding cars to enjoy the outdoors and save fuel (Chapter 7)

X-ray your house for energy leaks (Chapters 3, 7)

Yank weeds (Chapters 2, 3, 9)

Zealously share your love for God's world with family, friends, and neighbors (Chapter 10)

Have fun going green!

Be You and
Be Beautiful

So ... you might think "nature girl" is known for dirty fingernails and sweaty bandanas—she could never be the glam girl who's hanging out at the cosmetics counter, right? Not necessarily so! While it's fun to get gritty and grimy at times, girls who go green know how to make the most of their natural beauty.

If you're thinking, *I'm sooo not beautiful* or *I'm not a girly girl* ... strike that thought! Beauty starts from the inside, so let your inner sparkle glitter outward. Be truly beautiful by keeping your heart loving toward God, yourself, and others. Show kindness in your actions and words—that's the real beauty people see. No amount of makeup brightens your face like the flash of a great smile!

And know that every girl's best beauty secret weapon is ... self-confidence. Nothing is more attractive than a girl who holds herself in certainty—so stand up straight, make eye contact, and have faith that God has your back in every moment. God made you in total perfection, and it's his will (we swear!) that you love the way you look. That's a solemn promise, super-fox! So read on for some fun, all-natural ways to pamper yourself ...

> *"Your beauty should not come from outward adornment, such as elaborate hairstyles and the wearing of gold jewelry or fine clothes. Rather, it should be that of your inner self, the unfading beauty of a gentle and quiet spirit, which is of great worth in God's sight."*
>
> 1 PETER 3:3–4

Inner beauty is more important than outer beauty. I want my inner beauty to shine independence, strength, and kindness.

— HALEIGH, AGE 13, FLORIDA

Spa-day Spectacular!

Plan a fun at-home spa day for you and your friends to relax, refresh, and renew with your own homemade beauty treatments. We have loads of recipes for skin care products to make and try. But first, here are some ideas to make your spa day superbly special:

- **Set out a tray of natural flavors** to add to iced water. Try fresh mint leaves, citrus fruit slices, or strawberries. Let each girl mix her own drink.

- **Serve healthful snacks**, such as carrot-zucchini muffins, kale chips, and dipped strawberries (recipes in next chapter). And no paper products! Set out pretty plates, cloth napkins, and reusable cups. A blooming potted plant or vase of fresh flowers makes a nice centerpiece.

- **Play soft music and light scented soy candles** to set a mellow mood. Turn off all other electronics, such as the TV or your little brother's videogame (give him fair warning!).

- **Pray and share a favorite Bible verse**. Scripture can relax and bring joy. Psalm 23:2–3 reminds us that God restores our soul: *"He makes me lie down in green pastures, he leads me beside quiet waters, he refreshes my soul."*

- **Take a little time to sit outside** and enjoy God's beautiful creations. Listen to nature sounds with your eyes closed. Look closely at plants and trees—smell the leaves and blossoms. If it rains? Collect the water—rainwater is great for hair!

- **Make all-natural party favors**, such as bath-time potpourri pouches. Simply mix equal amounts of oatmeal, dried lavender, and rock salts in a bowl, then scoop onto cotton handkerchiefs. Bundle up and tie securely with ribbon or twine.

- **Make homemade beauty products,** such as glittery powders and gels (recipes on following pages), and have a blast applying them at your party.

Fabulous Facials!

Who doesn't love face painting? You'll flip for this beauty-mask treatment that's slathered on with a brush! Ingredients for masks and other recipes can be found at health food stores, drugstores, or online organic markets. For each girl, have one new soft-bristled paintbrush and three clean washcloths. Bacteria can grow on a damp washcloth, so use a fresh one each time.

1. Dip washcloth in warm scented water (recipes below). Cover face with the cloth and leave on for a minute or two to open pores.

2. Apply mask (recipes below) by smoothing a thin layer over face with paintbrush. Leave on five minutes max.

3. Dip a clean washcloth in warm water and remove mask, starting at forehead. Rinse face with water.

4. Dip another washcloth in scented water, and again cover face for one to two minutes. Relax, and enjoy how refreshed your face feels. Slowly roll the cloth down, starting at forehead.

5. Spritz face with scented water.

Tea Scented Water

What you need:

2 green tea bags
2 chamomile tea bags
Medium pot of warm water

What to do:

1. Steep tea bags in warm water three minutes.
2. Pour some of the water into a spritz bottle.

Lavender Scented Water

What you need:

6 cups warm water
Pure lavender oil

What to do:

1. Put two to four drops of lavender into water.
2. Pour some water into a spritz bottle.

Shelly's Yogurt Oatmeal and Honey Mask

This makes enough to share with about eight friends.

What you need:

¼ cup plain yogurt
½ cup oatmeal
2 tablespoons honey

What to do:

1. Mix together yogurt and honey in a medium bowl. Set aside.
2. Finely grind oatmeal in a blender, food processor, or coffee grinder, and add to yogurt mixture.

Shelly's Avocado Mask

This is for mixing up individually, enough for one treatment.

What you need:

¼ avocado
1 T. plain yogurt

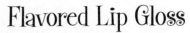

What to do:

1. Mash avocado in a bowl.
2. Stir in yogurt.

Flavored Lip Gloss

Pucker up, and blow God a big fruity-flavored kiss!

What you need:

1 tablespoon shortening (like Crisco) or un-petroleum jelly
Packet of sugar-free flavored drink mix
¼ cup hot water
Food glitter (with candy making supplies at craft store)
Olive oil, if needed

What to do:

1. Stir shortening or jelly in a bowl until it is soft and smooth. Add a few drops of olive oil to make it smoother, if needed. This is your base mixture.
2. In a different bowl, dissolve drink mix in hot water.
3. Add a few drops of the dissolved drink to the base mixture.
4. Store in a small container.

Be creative! Try different flavors — a sugar-free hot chocolate packet perhaps? Make up a name for your lips gloss like *Cherry Velvet* or *Lemon Zing*.

Glittery Dusting Powder

Make this ahead of time since it has to sit a couple days. Makes two cups.

What you need:

11 ounces tapioca starch
4 ounces baking soda
1 ounce kaolin (clay powder)
Cosmetic glitter
Vanilla oil
Cotton ball

What to do:

1. Combine starch, baking soda, and kaolin in a bowl.
2. Sprinkle in a tiny bit of cosmetic glitter.
3. Add 15 drops vanilla oil to cotton ball.
4. Place powder and pad in a glass jar with a tight lid.
5. Shake and stir the powder. Let sit 24 hours.
6. Shake and stir powder again, and let sit another 24 hours.
7. Discard cotton ball. Powder is ready to use.

Shelly's Body Glitter Gel

This is a fun project to make together during the party, then store in baby jars or other small containers for friends to take home.

What you need:

1 teaspoon un-petroleum jelly
4 teaspoons aloe vera gel
Ultrafine cosmetic-grade glitter

What to do:

1. Mix together un-petroleum jelly and aloe vera gel, and stir well.
2. Sprinkle a little glitter into your mixture. Stir again.
3. Test your creation on your hand to see how it looks.

4. If there's too much glitter, add more gel. Not enough glitter? Add more.
5. Place mixture into jar with spoon. Get sparkling!

Glitter gel sounds so cool—I would use that all the time.
— HALEIGH, AGE 13, FLORIDA

Shelly's Brown Sugar Foot Scrub

What you need:

2 T. brown sugar
2 T. ground oatmeal
2 T. aloe vera gel (or squeeze gel from a fresh plant)
1 tsp. fresh-squeezed lemon juice
1 T. honey
1 tsp. olive oil

What to do:

1. Mix ingredients together in a large bowl until mixture has a pasty texture.
2. Use a gentle circular motion to rub the paste onto heels, arches, soles, and toes.
3. Rinse feet with warm water.

Happy Feet!

The washing of feet was a significant act of respect in biblical times. Jesus washed his disciples' feet (John 13:5), and a woman poured perfume on Jesus's feet (John 12:3). So pay special attention to your tootsies at your spa party:

- **Soak feet in basins of warm water.** Add two tablespoons of baking soda and a few drops of a favorite essential oil to soothe.

- **Massage feet and legs** with a refreshing all-natural oil by mixing ½ cup almond oil or soy oil with four drops of peppermint oil.

- **Roll your foot over a tennis ball** for a do-it-yourself foot massage.

- **Give each other full-on pedicures** (and manicures). Be sure to try the recipe for Brown Sugar Foot Scrub, above.

Game: Beauty Blast! What's Your Secret?

Here's a great spa-party game—a fun way to share your favorite all-natural beauty tips with each other!

1. Have guests write their favorite beauty secrets—they must be all-natural, naturally!—on slips of paper, and toss them all into a bowl.

2. Take turns having each guest pull out a slip of paper and read it.

3. As each tip is read, try to guess which girl gave the tip.

4. Have the player who gave the tip explain it or add a little commentary (or even a demonstration!), like what makes it so easy to do or how often she uses it.

5. The winner is the person who gets the most tips matched up with the person who shared it.

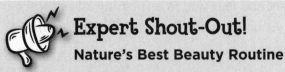

Expert Shout-Out!

Nature's Best Beauty Routine

Hey, gorgeous! We consulted a professional aesthetician for some great tips on how to be healthy and beautiful — *without* dropping a veritable fortune on expensive products and salon treatments you don't need. It's simple to enhance your God-given beauty...

- **Wash face** every morning and evening — clean skin is less prone to breakouts.

- **Zap zits** by mixing a packet of brewer's yeast with a few drops of lemon juice. Apply to affected area for 15 minutes, like a facial mask, to harden and push away gunk that clogs pores.

- **Drink lots** of water! Water hydrates skin from the inside out and flushes toxins.

- **Eat strawberries** or other berries for a natural (and tasty!) lip tint.

- **Take a bath** sprinkled with Epsom salts and a few drops of lavender oil to relax and soothe.

 • **Exfoliate hands** with the Brown Sugar Foot Scrub in this chapter.

- **Keep feet soft** (and warm) in cold weather. A few times a month, apply a lotion, then cover with socks and sleep in them.

- **Tame frizz** and make hair shine by rubbing olive oil in your palms and then through hair.

- **Help for oily hair**: Apply a small amount of cornstarch at crown, as close to hair roots and scalp as possible, and brush through hair. For dark hair, use a bronzing powder.

- **Eat healthfully** (see next chapter for some yummy healthful eating tips!) to keep skin, hair, and nails all-out lustrous, dah-ling.

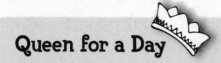

Queen for a Day

"Before a young woman's turn came to go to the king, she had to complete twelve months of beauty treatments prescribed for the women, six months with oil of myrrh and six with perfumes and cosmetics." (Esther 2:12)

Women and girls in biblical times relied on nature's secret ingredients when it came to primping and prettying themselves up. The Bible often refers to women's beauty, and personal cleanliness was important to most gals. Break out your Bible, and read about the beautiful young virgin Esther's "spa treatment" (Esther 2). She even won a beauty contest. Sort of.

Warning: Avoid These Ingredients

Even biblical women had to be careful of toxic elements, such as lead, when mixing up their "face paints." Check labels when buying beauty products, and avoid any that list the following:

- Talc—made from asbestos and is used in some powder products

- Fragrance/Parfum—could mean any of thousands of chemicals

- Parabens—toxic chemicals that trigger many allergic reactions

- Triclosan—found in some soaps and body washes, might do thyroid damage

- Compounds ending in "urea"—artificial preservatives that release formaldehyde
- Petrolatum byproduct—comes from gasoline production

What About Animal Testing?

Many cosmetics corporations used animals to test the safety of their products—that is, up until people protested and pointed to the practice as animal cruelty. Some cosmetics corporations now use the kinder  ToxCast, a computer program that predicts how chemicals will react with humans. But some hire a separate company to do their animal testing so they can claim they do not do it directly. And different countries have different rules. For example, China *requires* animal testing on cosmetics sold in their country, so  U.S. companies that sell products there must comply. Bottom line? The only way to know for sure is to do some online detective work about your favorite beauty brand.

✦ Real Girl ✦

Runaway Model

Lots of girls dream of becoming a fashion model, right? For Jennifer Strickland, that dream came true. At age 8, she began a modeling career that lasted into early adulthood. But guess what? Even as she strutted up and down designer runways and posed for fashion-magazine spreads, Jennifer didn't feel beautiful. Under pressure to look "perfect," Jennifer developed an eating disorder and became way too skinny. She finally found faith, discovering that God loves her and sees her true beauty within — no matter what. Jennifer learned to focus on physical and spiritual health, instead of outward appearance.

Jennifer now understands the real standard for beauty can't be found on the pages of a slick magazine — only in the magnificent heart of Christ. She discovered truth in Romans 1:21–23 that worshipping images is foolishness and darkens a person's heart. The only modeling Jennifer does now is role-modeling. She speaks to young girls about how to love themselves and really be beautiful inside and out — by loving themselves and God.

> **"I want teens to know they are more than how they compare to movie stars, the number of their friends on Facebook, and the images they see in magazines. They are uniquely gifted, valuable, and beautiful just for being who they are."**
>
> —Jennifer Strickland

If you feel you might have an eating disorder, never keep it a secret. Share your concerns with a trusted adult, such as a parent, school nurse, your favorite aunt, or a friend's mom. Seek others to help you develop a positive relationship with your body and food.

Quiz

What's Cookin', Good-lookin'?

Food fight!? Neh, but lots of random pantry items in your kitchen can be used as all-natural (and inexpensive) beauty treatments. See how well you're able to match up each food on the grocery list to the left with its cosmetic function, on the right:

1. Brown Sugar and Olive Oil
2. Banana Baby Food
3. Olive Oil and Garlic
4. Oatmeal
5. Epsom Salt
6. Honey and Cocoa Butter
7. Plain Yogurt
8. Raw Potato Slices
9. Mayonnaise and Honey
10. Avocado and Yogurt
11. Coffee Grounds and Water
12. Rosemary and Water
13. Castor Oil
14. Apple Cider Vinegar
15. Sea Salt and Baby Oil

a. Healthy Glow
b. Tighten Pores and Cleanse Skin
c. Exfoliate Skin
d. Relieve Aching Feet
e. Relieve Dry Skin
f. Soften Eyebrows
g. Soak for Healthy Nails
h. Hair Rinse
i. Rid Dark Under-eye Circles
j. Skin Toner
k. Lip Balm
l. Relieve Swollen Eyes
m. Soothe Sensitive Skin
n. Nourish Hair
o. Exfoliate Lips

Answer Key

1. o) Mix about ¼ teaspoon each brown sugar and olive oil in palm of hand, then gently rub a dab on your kisser to exfoliate lips.

2. i) Spread some banana baby food directly out of the jar under your eyes. Leave on for about 10 minutes and wash off. This helps rid dark under-eye circles.

3. g) Rub minced garlic on your nails and then put on some disposable gloves and leave gloves on for about 30 minutes to help strengthen nails.

4. m) Pour ⅓ cup of oatmeal into the foot part of a used nylon knee-high, and tie in a knot. Toss into warm bath water to soothe sensitive skin.

5. d) To relieve aching feet after a lot of walking or standing, dissolve ½ a cup of Epsom salt into ankle deep water in a tub and soak your tootsies for 20 minutes.

6. k) Rub ⅛ teaspoon each of cocoa butter and honey in your palm and rub it on your lips for a yummy lip balm.

7. b) Want to tighten pores and cleanse skin? Spread plain yogurt on your face, and wash it off after 10 minutes.

8. l) Don't put up with puffiness when you can relieve swollen eyes! Slice a raw potato into a couple of thin slices, then shut your eyes and place the potato slices on them for about 10 minutes.

9. n) Nourish hair by applying a mixture of ½ cup of mayonnaise and 3 tablespoons of honey. Start at the end of hair, work toward the roots. Leave in for 15 to 30 minutes before shampooing.

10. e) Use a weekly avocado and yogurt facial mask to relieve dry skin (see recipe earlier in the chapter).

11. a) Get a healthy glow by mixing used coffee grounds with a little warm water and rubbing in light circular motions on your face. Rinse off after about a minute.

12. h) Heat some fresh rosemary in a pan of water (use rainwater if possible), just enough to cover the herb, and simmer for 10 minutes. Strain so you end up with just scented water. Use as a hair rinse after you shampoo and condition to give it a healthy shine.

13. f) Soften eyebrows by using a cotton swab to dab on a little castor oil.

14. j) Soak a cotton ball with apple cider vinegar, then swipe on clean face for a refreshing skin toner.

15. c) Mix ½ a cup of sea salt with ¼ cup of baby oil. Put it into a covered container to sit for 24 hours. Massage this homemade skin softener onto rough skin areas, then shower off.

Eco-Careers

Health and Beauty

- **Environmental Health and Safety Technician**

  "I help keep people safe at their jobs!"

- **Toxicologist**

  "I work to make beauty products safe for you."

- **Aesthetician**

  "My job is to help people choose the right skin care."

- **Dietician**

  "I give advice on how to have a good balanced diet."

chapter 2

You Are What You Eat

When you and your family take a trip through the grocery store, are you conscious about choosing good-for-you foods? Or do you toss lots of junk snacks loaded with sugars, sodium, and dyes into your cart? There were no drive-thrus or food factories during the biblical era, so dinner was *never* served from a cardboard box. Most meals were made up of fresh fruits, vegetables, whole grains, nuts, seeds, olives, fish, and honey. Everything was organic. All natural!

Not only are organic foods better for you, but organic farming uses less chemicals than traditional methods and is safer for the earth too! Organic foods are certainly available today, whether you shop at a food chain, local farmers' market, or grow rows of cherry tomatoes and sugar-snap peas in your backyard. Even if you'd prefer a drippy slice of pizza over a steamy bowl of lentil soup or would rather stuff your mouth with mini-marshmallows than a handful of figs, you just might find that you actually (gulp) *enjoy* chowing down on nature's foods. Read on, hungry girl ...

"So whether you eat or drink or whatever you do, do it all for the glory of God."

1 Corinthians 11:31

Eat all your healthy food first, then you will only be hungry enough to eat a little junk food.

— Madeline, age 10, Maryland

Healthy Soil = Healthful Food

Good food depends on the health of the soil. So ... organic farmers use natural forms of fertilizer— and that usually means animal manure! Sounds yucky, but it greatly enriches the soil. The richer soil contains more worms and microbes, and makes healthier crops.

The farm animals are fed from those crops—then the animals' manure goes into the soil and the cycle continues ...

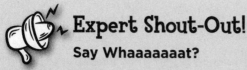 ## Expert Shout-Out!
Say Whaaaaaaat?

So what exactly is "organic food" anyway? Well, it's pretty good stuff. Here's a mini lesson from the U.S. Department of Agriculture on what it means when you see organic on the menu...

- Organic food is produced by farmers who emphasize the use of renewable resources and the conservation of soil and water to enhance environmental quality for future generations.

- Organic meat, poultry, eggs, and dairy products come from animals that are given no antibiotics or growth hormones.

- Organic food is produced without using most conventional pesticides, fertilizers made with synthetic ingredients or sewage sludge, bioengineering, or ionizing radiation.

- Before a product can be labeled "*organic*," the farm where the food is grown is inspected to make sure the farmer is following all the rules necessary to meet organic standards.

- Companies that handle or process organic food before it gets to your local supermarket or restaurant must be certified, too.

Why Buy Local? Local food, grown within one hundred miles of your home, is fresher when you buy it. It also saves energy due to lower transportation costs and helps farmers earn more money. Scope out local produce that's in season, and look for other foods that are produced in your area.

Eat Your Veggies!

When the prophet Daniel was imprisoned, he refused to eat the daily portion of rich royal food and wine that was brought to him. The prison guard pleaded with him to eat, so Daniel struck up a bargain for himself and the other prisoners: "'Please test us for ten days: Give us nothing but vegetables to eat and water to drink. Then compare our appearance with that of the young men who eat the royal food, and treat your servants in accordance with what you see.... At the end of the ten days they looked healthier and better nourished than any of the young men who ate the royal food. So the guard took away their choice food and the wine they were to drink and gave them vegetables instead." (Daniel 1:12 – 13, 15)

Be a Food Detective

Ever wonder how much fat is in the mystery meat inside those cans of pasta you like to eat straight from the can? Or how much refined sugar is in that box of artificially fruit-flavored and multi-colored cereal you munch in the a.m.? Turn to the back of food packages, and read the ingredients. See all those words you can't even pronounce? Many of those are artificial compounds and man-made chemicals—in your food! Do your research, and know what you're putting in your body. Here's an experiment you can do now to get a clue:

Contents Under Pressure

This gives you a visual for breaking down the amount of fat, sugar, and vitamins in your favorite foods.

What you need:

Food package
Measuring spoon
Sugar
Shortening
Clear cups
Water

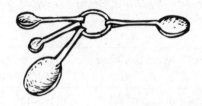

What to do:

1. Read the nutrition facts labeled on a package of food, such as your favorite brand of cookies.
2. For each gram of sugars per serving, measure and pour ¼ teaspoon of sugar into a cup.
3. For each gram of total fat per serving, measure ¼ teaspoon of shortening into a second cup.
4. For each gram of sodium per serving, measure ¼ teaspoon of salt into another cup.
5. Note the percentage of vitamins and minerals in each one and list them. For each one percent of a vitamin, pour ¼ teaspoon of water into a glass and label it for that vitamin.
6. Look at the glasses and you'll see how much of each item is in the food. Hopefully, there's more water than sugar, fat, or sodium.

Be a Vitamins and Minerals Diva!

What's the big deal about vitamins and minerals? Um, you need them to live—and thrive. Sure, maybe you're in the habit of popping a daily chewable multi-vitamin as part of your daily routine. Cool. But fact is, every nutrient your body needs is found in the foods God has given us.

Want great-looking skin? These vitamins and minerals will help:

Name	Where to find it
Vitamin A: Retinol and Beta-carotene	Sweet potatoes, carrots, pumpkin, milk, liver, whole eggs
Vitamin C: Ascorbic Acid	Citrus fruits, bright colored fruits and vegetables, kiwi
Vitamin D: group of fat soluble vitamins (can be absorbed in fat but not in water)	Bodies manufacture this from direct exposure to the sun or you can eat fortified foods like cereal and milk
Vitamin E: Tocopherol	Vegetable oils, nuts, whole wheat products, egg yolks, and green leafy vegetables

Trying to balance out your body weight? Work on the rate your body digests and burns food with these vitamins and minerals:

Name	Where to find it
Vitamin B2: Riboflavin	Leafy green vegetables, tomatoes, almonds, beans, and cheese
Vitamin B3: Niacin	Chicken, beef, fish, avocado, broccoli, nuts, and eggs
Vitamin B5: Pantothenic Acid	Meats, whole grains, broccoli, and avocado
Vitamin H	Yeast, eggs, dairy, fish
Iodine	Saltwater fish, seaweed, shellfish, and iodized salt

Want to think better? Try these foods:

Name	Where to find it
Vitamin B1: Thiamine	Flax, asparagus, potatoes, cauliflower, and eggs
Sodium (Salt)	Naturally found in many foods and added to others

The following minerals help strengthen your bones:

Name	Where to find it
Calcium	Milk, dairy products, leafy green vegetables, beans, shellfish, and tofu
Copper	Shellfish, whole grains, beans, and dried fruit

Want to prevent cramping and help your blood cells grow? Then try these:

Name	Where to find it
Vitamin B6: Pyridoxine	Fish, liver, beef, starchy vegetables, and non-citrus fruits
Vitamin B12: Cyanocobalamin	Clams, beef, liver, fish, poultry, and eggs
Vitamin K	Dark green leafy vegetables, eggs, cheese, pork, and liver
Potassium	Bananas, tomatoes, potatoes, dried fruit, raw vegetables, mushrooms, fish, and milk

Do you get tired easily or feel stressed? The following vitamins up your energy level:

Name	Where to find it
Vitamin B9: Folic Acid	Leafy vegetables, beans, and sunflower seeds
Vitamin M: Folate	Vegetables, whole wheat, beans, and mushrooms
Iron	Red meats, whole wheat, shellfish, nuts, and dried fruit

Home-Cooked Cuisine

Some people think it's too much trouble to make food from scratch, but it's easy if you're patient. Farmers know the importance of patience as they must wait for seeds to grow and produce food …

"Be patient, then, brothers and sisters, until the Lord's coming. See how the farmer waits for the land to yield its valuable crop, patiently waiting for the autumn and spring rains." (James 5:7)

So get in the kitchen, break out the cooking supplies, and have some culinary fun! Cute vintage apron, optional.

How to Churn Butter

Fill a jar halfway with heavy cream.
Put the lid on tight, and shake it
for ten minutes. (Feel free to crank
up the music and dance around the
kitchen as you shake!) Shaking the
cream causes the fat and protein to stick
together and form butter. A larger and
larger chunk will form. Scoop it out. The
remaining liquid is buttermilk, which you can use
in the smoothie recipe below …

Buttermilk Fruit Smoothie

*Experiment with your favorite fruits. If a smoothie needs
to be thicker, add banana slices. Too thick? Toss in a few
ice cubes and blend again.*

What you need:

1½ cups sliced fresh strawberries
½ cup buttermilk
¼ cup fresh-squeezed orange juice
1 tablespoon honey

What to do:

1. Dump all ingredients into a blender.
2. Cover and blend until smooth, about a minute or two.
3. Pour into chilled glasses, and enjoy!

Jesus the Bread of Life

They found him on the other side of the lake. They asked him, "Rabbi, when did you get here?"

Jesus answered, "What I'm about to tell you is true. You are not looking for me because you saw miraculous signs. You are looking for me because you ate the loaves until you were full. Do not work for food that spoils. Work for food that lasts forever. That is the food the Son of Man will give you. God the Father has put his seal of approval on him."

Then they asked him, "What does God want from us? What works does he want us to do?"

Jesus answered, "God's work is to believe in the One he has sent."

So they asked him, "What miraculous sign will you give us? What will you do so we can see it and believe you? Long ago our people ate the manna in the desert. It is written in Scripture, "The Lord gave them bread from heaven to eat.'"

Jesus said to them, "What I'm about to tell you is true. It is not Moses who has given you the bread from heaven. It is my Father who gives you the true bread from heaven. The bread of God is the One who comes down from heaven. He gives life to the world."

"Sir," they said, "give us this bread from now on."

Then Jesus said, "I am the bread of life. No one who comes to me will ever go hungry. And no one who believes in me will ever be thirsty. But it is just as I told you. You have seen me, and you still do not believe." (John 6:25–36, NIrV)

Honey-of-an-Egg Whole-Wheat Bread

Jesus often broke bread with his friends, and so did early Christians! This recipe makes two loaves or 24 large "Trinity rolls."

What you need:

1 package yeast
1 cup warm water
3 eggs
1 cup warm milk (microwave it one minute)
¼ cup honey
¼ cup oil
6 cups whole-wheat flour
3 tsp. salt

What to do:

1. Let yeast dissolve in water in a small bowl for ten minutes. Set a timer since this is important in helping the bread rise.
2. Stir eggs, milk, honey, and oil in a large bowl.
3. Add the yeast and water (after the ten minutes is done).
4. Add salt, and stir in flour one cup at a time. You might only need 5½ cups. If dough seems very stiff, set the remaining flour aside to use when you knead the dough. (Kneading is when you push and massage the dough to mix in air.)
5. Turn dough into a greased bowl, cover with a dish-towel, and set in a warm spot until doubled, one to two hours.
6. Check the dough, and make sure it has about doubled. It should be higher in the middle and twice as much as what you had before. Gently press two fingers into the center of the dough. When you can still see the holes you made, the dough is ready.

(continued)

7. Punch down the dough. This means to make a fist (grease your fist), then push down in the center of the mound of dough.
8. Dump the dough onto a floured board or tabletop, and knead. Push the dough and roll it, turn it a bit and push again. Keep doing this for five minutes. The bread will be softer because of the kneading.
9. Place in a floured and greased loaf pan, or shape the bread into rolls. For Trinity rolls, pull off small hunks of dough and roll into balls about one inch in size. Put three balls into each section of a muffin tin. This represents the three persons in one God, the Trinity.
10. Let the dough sit again to rise a second time. Let it sit 20 minutes.
11. Bake loaf at 350 for 50 to 60 minutes; bake rolls 35 to 40 minutes.

Easy-Cheesy Stuffed Zucchini

Whether you pick up ingredients at a local farmers' market or grow your own, have a fun time cooking up something from the garden.

What you need:

6 plain crackers
1 tablespoon dried cranberries
2 teaspoons chopped fresh parsley
1 teaspoon bacon bits
1 tablespoon butter (churn your own!)
¼ cup shredded cheese
1 zucchini

What to do:

1. Preheat oven to 400 degrees.
2. Turn crackers to fine crumbs by putting them in a zipper-lock plastic bag and smashing with a rolling pin or crushing with your hands.

3. Put cranberries, parsley, and bacon bits in plastic bag with cracker crumbs.
4. Crumble butter into the mixture, and continue to mix it in until butter is spread throughout. Add cheese, and again blend it well with your hands.
5. Cut zucchini in half, and scoop out and discard seeds (or dry them and use for planting, see instructions below).
6. Put ½ of crumb mixture into each half of the zucchini.
7. Place stuffed zucchini in a baking pan that has been sprayed with cooking spray.
8. Cook in oven for 10 minutes, or until top is browned.

Zee Zucchini Zeeds!

The seeds you scoop out from your zucchini recipe, above, can be dried and planted. Try this with other fruits and veggies too!

What you need:

Zucchini (or vegetable with seeds)
Piece of clean cheesecloth or paper towel
Paper bag or empty envelope

What to do:

1. Cut the zucchini open. If the zucchini is mature, the seeds are larger and you can pick them out one at a time and place on cloth or towel to dry.
2. If seeds are small, the zucchini is younger. Scoop out seeds, and place in a colander. Quickly run water over the seeds and stringy insides. Separate the seeds out, and place on cloth to dry.
3. Drying might take a few days or even weeks, depending on how wet the seeds are and how humid or dry the air is in your home. Once completely dry, store the seeds in an envelope or paper bag (not plastic as that will hold in moisture) until ready to plant.

Tangy Tomato Sauce

Use this sauce to make English Muffin Pizzas (recipe opposite), over your favorite pasta, or as a dipping sauce for whole-grain chips. You can use tomatoes that are a bit older — it's a great way to use up tomatoes that didn't get eaten while they were fresh.

What you need:

2 large tomatoes
2 teaspoons salt, divided
2 tablespoons olive oil, divided
1 teaspoon chopped parley
1 teaspoon chopped basil
1 teaspoon chopped oregano

What to do:

1. Preheat oven to 300 degrees.
2. Cut tomatoes into quarters.
3. Cover a baking sheet with aluminum foil.
4. Place tomatoes, cut side up, on the sheet.
5. Sprinkle ½ tsp. salt and 1 T. oil over the tomatoes.
6. Cook for 20 minutes, then remove from oven and use tongs to turn tomatoes over. While holding each tomato with the tongs, use a fork to pull the skin off the tomato pieces and discard the skin.
7. Sprinkle remaining salt and oil on the tomatoes.
8. Put them back into the oven for another 20 minutes.
9. Take the tomatoes out of the oven and put them in a pot. Use a hand blender to puree (cause the tomatoes to become a smooth liquid) the tomatoes.
10. Stir the parsley, basil, and oregano into the liquid and cook over medium-low heat for ten minutes.

English Muffin Pizzas

What you need:

Tomato sauce (recipe across)
Shredded mozzarella
English muffin
Favorite toppings

What to do:

1. Preheat oven or toaster oven to 400 degrees.
2. Break English muffin in half.
3. Spread tomato sauce on each side of the muffin.
4. Add toppings, then cover with cheese.
5. Bake for about 12 minutes, or until cheese is melted and lightly browned.

Carrot-Zucchini Muffins

Use the same recipe to make strawberry or blueberry muffins. Simply omit the grated veggies and cheese, and substitute ¾ cup chopped strawberries or whole blueberries. Makes one dozen.

What you need:

1½ cup flour
½ cup sugar
1 teaspoon cinnamon
2½ tsp. baking powder
¼ tsp. salt
½ cup grated carrot
½ cup grated zucchini
½ cup shredded cheddar (optional)
1 egg, beaten
⅓ cup canola oil
¼ cup milk

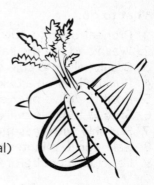

(continued)

What to do:

1. Preheat oven to 350 degrees.
2. Mix together dry ingredients and set aside.
3. Beat together egg, oil, veggies, and cheese.
4. Add in dry ingredients, and stir just enough to mix and moisten flour mix (15–20 strokes at most).
5. Place liners into muffin tin, and fill two-thirds full.
6. Bake 20 minutes. Let cool slightly before removing from tin.

Kale Chips

This is a goodness-packed snack and sneaky way to get your greens! Play around with other seasonings to make different flavored chips. Store up to two days in a sealed container.

What you need:

1 cup kale, packed
1 T. olive oil
1 tsp. seasoned salt
1 tsp. paprika

What to do:

1. Preheat oven to 300 degrees.
2. Wash and dry the kale.
3. Break kale into chip size pieces.
4. Put the kale on a baking sheet.
5. Pour the olive oil over the kale.
6. Spread the kale out on the sheet.
7. Sprinkle with seasoned salt and paprika.
8. Bake for 10 minutes or until edges are lightly browned.
9. Let chips cool before eating.

Dipped Strawberries

This is a tasty way to enjoy strawberries or any other fruit that's good for dipping—try it with banana slices, orange segments, or apple wedges.

What you need:

Fresh strawberries
½ cup vanilla yogurt
Toppings (crushed nuts, coconut,
   crushed graham crackers, cocoa powder)

What to do:

1. Rinse strawberries under running water, and pat dry with paper towel.
2. Put ¼ cup of each topping in separate bowls.
3. Dip strawberries in the yogurt and then in a topping. Eat up!

✨ Real Girl ✨

City Slicker to Country Gal

Karen Dakin grew up in the city and didn't know how to farm. She only knew that fruits, vegetables, milk, and meat came from stores. Her first visit to a farm had her holding her nose from the smells. And the big cows scared her. Now, she and her husband own a huge sustainable dairy farm. She found out it takes a lot of work to care for the land and cows, but she loves it. She makes sure the cows are well-fed and washed. She also knows that God wants her to farm. It turned out that his plans for her were not what she expected when she was young. Pray and ask God to direct your life. And he will …

Quiz

Food For Thought

Many foods do much more than fill your belly and satisfy your hunger — they have sneaky super-powers! See if you can guess the following foods' best-kept secrets...

1. Mushrooms
   a. Are good for your boobs
   b. Make great homes for little creatures
   c. Help you to mush your dogs

2. Yogurt
   a. Helps you run faster
   b. Is an awesome after-dinner dessert
   c. Provides a good source of fruit

3. Eggs
   a. Help the Easter Bunny fill your basket
   b. Could boost your grades
   c. Are great for tossing

4. Kiwi
   a. Is one of the world's most healthful fruits
   b. Are adorable birds from Australia
   c. Turn your tongue a great shade of green

5. Quinoa (pronounced *keen-wa*)
   a. Is good for keeping energy levels up
   b. Makes your jeans fit better
   c. Both a and b

6. Salmon
   a. Leaves your house smelling wonderful
   b. Protects your heart
   c. Provides great exercise while catching them

7. Broccoli

    a. Makes your bones stronger

    b. Lets cute little trees grow in your stomach

    c. Both a and b

8. Sweet potatoes

    a. Are a great way to keep from eating white potatoes

    b. Give your skin a healthy glow

    c. Are like white potatoes with added sugar

9. Blueberries

    a. Keep you full longer

    b. Make your teeth stronger and blue

    c. Are a great source of vitamin C

10. Almonds

    a. Have a nice licorice taste

    b. Give a healthy boost to blood flow

    c. Are only to be eaten on Mondays

11. Avocados

    a. Are low in fat

    b. Add a great crunch to your guacamole

    c. Could lengthen your life span

12. Kale

    a. Is fun to collect while at the beach

    b. Could keep your peepers in tip-top shape

    c. Would make a great sail on a model boat

Answer Key

1. a. Eating mushrooms helps protect against breast cancer.

2. b. Yogurt helps your digestive system work better.

3. b. Eggs provide the vitamin choline, which is good for brain development and memory.

4. a. Kiwis are a great source of potassium, as well as vitamins A and E.

5. c. Quinoa is a grain that's a good source of iron and protein, *and* helps control your weight and reduce your risk for heart disease.

6. b. Salmon helps protect your heart with omega–3 fatty acids.

7. a. Broccoli has bone-building vitamin K and calcium.
8. b. Sweet potatoes are loaded with vitamin A, which is great for skin.
9. a. The water and fiber in blueberries help keep you full longer.
10. b. Almonds keep blood vessels healthy.
11. c. Avocados lower cholesterol, contributing to a longer life.
12. b. Kale is a good source of lutein, which benefits the eyes.

Eco-Careers

Food Industry

- **Agricultural Inspector**

  "I inspect farms, fisheries, and other places where food is grown or harvested."

- **Rancher**

  "I operate machinery and raise animals for food."

- **Food Science Technician**

  "I measure and analyze the quality of food."

- **Agricultural Scientist**

  "I find new safer ways to grow food and help farmers produce more food with less land."

Be an Earth BFF

Once, there was a place where no one could live ... or even take a stroll. Years of manufacturing nuclear weapons contaminated the land, as harmful waste leaked into the ground. Finally, the factory was closed down by the government. Scientists expected that no animal or person would be able to inhabit the area for decades. Oops ... wrong!

Within ten years, the land became a thriving home for wild animals. People are still not allowed there, but elk, Preble's meadow jumping mice, painted turtles, birds, prairie dogs, and other animals roam the land and live there. It's called Rocky Flats, in Colorado, and it's now habitable because people cared and worked to clean up the toxins from the soil—and because God made the world able to heal itself.

God wants us to partner with him to make the earth beautiful. Choose to care for the earth, one plot of ground at a time. Rejoice when you succeed at making our planet more beautiful. Here's a verse to reminds us that God sends his helper, the Holy Spirit, to team with us on renewing the earth ...

> *"When you send your Spirit, they are created, and you renew the face of the ground."*
>
> PSALM 104:30

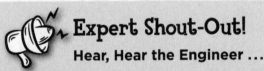

Expert Shout-Out!
Hear, Hear the Engineer ...

An engineer from the Defense Nuclear Facilities Safety Board shared this information about how experts are trying to figure out the best ways to prevent wastelands:

- **Not just sci-fi!** Engineers study what will happen in the future as a result of what we do today. They understand we need to recycle materials and restore the earth, so they're testing and making better decisions before building new factories or equipment.

- **It's best to prevent problems.** Just like putting books neatly in a bookcase prevents a stack of books from becoming a landslide, so too, engineers work to offset problems *before* they happen. Newer designs and controls prevent future environmental accidents.

- **Nuclear waste can't just be tossed** out because it is harmful. The waste is stored in very safe containers far beneath the earth's surface in old abandoned mines. Engineers designed containers to last longer than it takes for uranium (the radioactive element that creates nuclear energy) to decay.

The Scoop on Poop

Think about waste you can help get rid of safely, like animal waste (poop). Yucky thought, but it's part of owning a cute furry critter. Pet waste is a real problem because many pets eat meat, so their waste contains many germs and parasites. Yep, it's official—dog poop is considered a toxic element, according to the Environmental Protection Agency. The safest way to get rid of dog poop? Flush it down the toilet! There are even flushable bags made especially for doggie doo.

But wait a minute! Why is it that cow manure is *good* for the earth while dog poop is not? It's because cows chow on plants and aren't meat-eaters. Cow dung is made of methane gas, carbon dioxide, phosphorous, and sulfur, making the soil richer and better for growing plants.

Here's the Dirt ...

Who knew you could help keep the planet squeaky clean by getting down and dirty? Sure, there's a lot of ground to cover—but you can do your part just by focusing on your little piece of the planet. Keep reading for some really fun, earth-lovin' projects. Be prepared to get good and grimy!

How Does Your Garden Grow?

You can make a difference now by finding a piece of land that needs some lovin'—maybe a deserted lot or perhaps your elderly neighbor's neglected garden. Surrounded by cement and sidewalks? Not a problem! You can still get something growing ...

- **Take a "before" photo** of your adopted plot of land. Let adults inspect the land and remove anything dangerous. Put on work gloves. Remove trash and topsoil that contains oil or other pollutants. Add fertilizer, compost, or other nutrients to make the soil more healthy.

- **During World War II**, people planted victory gardens on dry, weedy patches of land. The vegetable gardens produced million tons of food for hungry people in Europe. Try planting something you can eat.

- **Plant an indoor container** of pea pods or cherry tomatoes, moving it outside to a porch or patio as weather permits. When they grow, you can pluck your own snack right from the vine!

- **For a bean teepee**, plant a few seeds in the center of a container of soil. Place three sticks, evenly spaced, at the edge of the soil and tie them together at the top to form the teepee frame. Let the bean plant send off shoots to climb the sticks.

- **Plant a window box of herbs** to grow and snip off your own seasonings as needed.

- **Plant edible flowers** like pansies (taste minty) or day lilies (taste like asparagus).

- **Plant magic bean sprouts.** Rinse ½ cup dried Mung beans, place in bottom of a

Ever wonder what makes seeds grow? We can plant seeds in good soil and water and care for them, but we can't make the seed sprout and grow. God causes that to happen. Plant those seeds and let God work his miracle of growth. That's a good reminder that we need to let go of what we can't force to happen and pray for God to bring about the change.

Night and day the seed comes up and grows. It happens whether the farmer sleeps or gets up. He doesn't know how it happens. (Mark 4:27)

glass jar, and pour in several inches of water. Cover the jar with a piece of cheesecloth held in place with a rubber band and soak overnight. The next day drain the water, rinse beans, and recover. Rinse beans twice daily and drain water. Eat the yummy sprouts that grow!

- **Create weed barriers** with old newspaper or copy paper by placing sheets of the paper around plants as mulch. Replace when it decomposes.

"I love the idea of growing our own food because it's always right there. Peppers? Be a dear and run outside. Watermelon? Just grab a big one from the back yard. I like farmers' markets because everything tastes better without the packaging and spraying and all that.
— AINSLEY, AGE 11, MARYLAND

Toil in the Soil

Before you begin your garden, try to identify the type of soil you have. Then, test your soil for certain factors that will affect how well your garden thrives (soil testing instructions to follow).

First, moisten the soil. Squeeze a handful with your fist, then open your hand and poke the soil with your finger:

- **If the soil holds the shape from your fist and then crumbles** … you probably have good soil for planting.

- **If the soil holds it shape and does not crumble easily** … it contains clay. Dig up and remove clay so soil can drain, and add compost. Compost is a mixture of decayed plants and natural materials such as leaves, manure, and vegetable scraps. There's more about compost in this chapter, so read on.

- **If the soil doesn't hold its shape** … it is sandy soil. Mix in lots of compost to sandy soil.

Soil Test for pH factor

The pH factor is the measure of acidity (sourness) or basicity (opposite of acid) in the soil. A soil of high basicity is called alkaline. This test will help you know if the soil has a pH problem.

What you need:
Small shovel or scoop
Two plastic cups
White vinegar
Baking soda

What to do:
1. Scoop some soil into each cup.
2. Add ½ cup vinegar to one cup. If you see fizzes or bubbles, the soil is alkaline. Lilacs and clematis like to grow in alkaline soil.
3. Add ¼ distilled water to 1 cup soil and stir to make mud. Stir in ¼ cup baking soda. If the soil mix bubbles or fizzes, it is acidic. Azaleas and blueberries like acidic soil. But many plants will be hard to grow in that soil, unless you lower the acidity with limestone or ashes from a fireplace or woodstove.

Soil Drainage Test

Soil drainage, or permeability, is how fast or slow water flows through the soil. If it flows off too fast the plants will not get enough water. If the water stays too long the plants sit in too much water and can drown.

What you need:

Large shovel
Water

What to do:

1. Dig a hole one foot deep, about a six-inch circumference, and fill it with water.
2. Let the water drain out of the hole.
3. Fill the hole again, and time how long it takes to drain.
4. If it takes more than four hours, the soil has poor drainage. Clay holds the water in the soil (like a glass holds water), and the water sits too long for most plants. If there's lots of clay you need to dig it up and remove it. Then add compost.
5. If it drains in less than an hour, the soil may be too sandy or full of gravel and rocks that don't hold in the water. The water flows through too fast for plants to grow well. If so, you may need to add compost to the soil to help it hold the water better.

Worm Test

Maybe worms make you squirm, but when it comes to healthy soil—worms are your friends!

What you need:

Large shovel
Piece of plastic or cardboard

What to do:

1. Dig up one square foot of warm soil (at least 55 degrees) and dump it on a piece of plastic or cardboard.

2. Count the number of worms in the soil. Less than ten means there's not enough organic matter in the soil, or the pH factor isn't good (the soil is too acidic or too alkaline). At least ten worms means the soil is rich in organisms and good for growing plants.

Eco-Fun! How to Make a Compost Pile

Composting uses food scraps to keep soil healthy. Composting also adds good microbes and bacteria to the soil that help plants naturally fight off pests. At first your pile will be lumpy, but after several weeks, it will break down and turn into a rich soil.

First, you need a place to put the scraps. You can either have a parent help you enclose an area (doesn't need a bottom) with some wood and chicken wire, or you can use an old garbage can that you poke lots of small holes in both the bottom and sides. If you build a container, it should be about one yard wide, long, and high.

What you need:

1. Nitrogen, found in green yard clippings like grass, bush trimmings, vegetable and fruit matter, as well as animal poop.
2. Carbon, which is the brown part from dry leaves, twigs, untreated wood sawdust, and hay. Nothing you add should be longer than twelve inches. For faster composting, chop or shred items.
3. Air is needed to keep the pile from getting dense by fluffing it. You fluff the pile by turning it over a few times with a pitchfork or metal rake.
4. Water helps the microbes and bacteria work. The compost pile needs to stay moist. You can check the moisture by pulling out a handful of material from the middle of the pile and squeezing it—if a few drops of water come out it is good. When you need to add water either put a hose in the middle of the pile or water as you turn the compost to add air.

The Secret's in the Soil

Jesus told this famous parable about a farmer scattering seeds. The seeds were good but not all grew into healthy and fruitful plants because the soil made a difference…

"A farmer went out to sow his seed. As he was scattering the seed, some fell along the path; it was trampled on, and the birds ate it up. Some fell on rocky ground, and when it came up, the plants withered because they had no moisture. Other seed fell among thorns, which grew up with it and choked the plants. Still other seed fell on good soil. It came up and yielded a crop, a hundred times more than was sown." (Luke 8:5–8)

The point of this parable? The seed represents God's word, and the soil is our heart. We want our hearts to be healthy so God's word can grow within us.

Keeping equal amounts of brown and green material, along with checking the moisture and fluffing the pile, will make a difference in how fast new dirt forms. It can take three to ten months.

Problems that might come up and their solutions

1. **It's smelly!** Either the pile is too wet and you need to add dry ingredients, or there is not enough air and you need to turn the pile.
2. **It's too cool.** In order for the microbes to work the pile needs to get very hot (over one hundred degrees). The pile may be too dry (add water); too small (add more material into it); or lack nitrogen (add green stuff); or pieces within the pile are too big (chop them up).
3. **Oh no!** Rats or other pests in the compost … This usually means the pile has bones, fatty or starchy food, or animal poo in it. Move these items to the center of the pile where they cannot be smelled as easily, or avoid adding such items to the compost pile.

Stupendous Seed Strips

Time to get growing! These strips that have seeds attached make planting easier—and they make great gifts for gardeners.

What you need:

Packet of seeds, any variety
One-inch wide strips of newspaper, thick paper towels, or
　　other biodegradable paper
1 cup flour
½ cup water
Plant fertilizer or plant food granules
Popsicle sticks
Marker

What to do:

1. Write the name of the seed on the strip of paper. Turn it over so the name will show on the outside when the strip is later rolled up.
2. Read the seed packet to see how far apart the seeds should be planted. Using the marker, mark the distance on the strips of paper.
3. Mix the flour and water to make a paste. Use about twice the amount of flour as water. Only a little of the mixture is needed for each seed. Put a dab on each mark on the paper and then place a seed on the paste. Add a little fertilizer next to each seed.
4. Let paste dry.
5. Mark the popsicle stick with the name of the plant. Also, write how deep to plant the seeds. For shallow plantings, mark the depth to plant on the stick.
6. To plant, dig a trench the correct depth for the seeds and lay out the strip. Cover the strip with soil, and water until moist but not drenched. Trust God to provide the rain and sunshine needed.

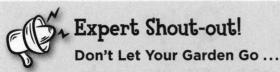

Expert Shout-out!

Don't Let Your Garden Go ...

Continue to care for your garden by following these easy (but necessary!) steps. Here are some tips from a certified plant professional:

- **Water, weed, and fertilize** as needed. If you get confused, go to a local nursery or garden center and ask for advice.

- **Chase away garden pests**. Plant marigolds to deter harmful insects. Sprinkle used coffee grounds to keep snails and beetles away. Eggshells (rinsed and crumbled) chase away slugs. Plant garlic to repel bugs. Make a garlic spray by adding a few cloves of garlic in a bottle with water.

- **Invite garden helpers** like ladybugs (they eat aphids and other harmful plant pests) and butterflies (they pollinate the flowers). Ladybugs like plants with broad, umbrella type leaves for landing on and yellow or white flowers like bright marigolds and scented geraniums. Butterflies like bright colors and native plants.

- **Keep deer away** from the garden by pulling hair out of your brush and spreading it around plants, or put out pieces of fragranced soap.

Me love aphids!

Quiz

How Green Are You?

Take this quiz now to test your knowledge about going green. Retake it when you finish the book to see how much you've learned. Choose the correct meaning for each "going green" word or phrase below.

1. Recycle
   a. Take another bicycle ride
   b. A new life cycle
   c. To use again

2. Forest sustainability
   a. A tough grass or tree stain that won't wash out
   b. Process that helps trees in the woods last
   c. How long you can camp in the woods

3. Environment
   a. Everything around you living or not
   b. Living things around you
   c. A sweet-tasting candy

4. Hydroponic
   a. A new way to learn to read
   b. Tool for hearing under water
   c. Growing plants in water and nutrients, without soil

5. Acid rain
   a. Music from a rock band
   b. A chemistry experiment that smells bad
   c. Rain that contains bad chemicals

6. Climate
   a. To go up a mountain
   b. Usual weather in a region
   c. Bad weather

7. Endangered
   a. At risk of becoming extinct
   b. In an unsafe place
   c. Mom's threats when you don't obey

8. Conservation
   a. Talking to people
   b. Careful use of resources
   c. Space in hotels

9. Pollution
   a. When bees gather nectar from flowers
   b. Man-made waste in air, water, or soil
   c. A tug of war

10. Polystyrene
    a. A loud siren
    b. A new style of clothes
    c. Tough plastic material used in making packaging

11. Ecological footprint
    a. Tracks animals make
    b. Tracks made by a group of people
    c. Average amount of air, soil, and water a person uses

12. Water cycle
    a. How much water is used in one day
    b. A paddleboat you pedal in the water
    c. Continuous movement of water (evaporation, condensation, precipitation)

13. Oxygen cycle
    a. How much air you breathe in and out
    b. The exchange of oxygen people and animals breathe in and carbon dioxide they breathe out, combined with oxygen trees give off and carbon dioxide trees absorb.
    c. A new type of bike with a motor that uses air

14. Compost
    a. A common post for a fence
    b. Mix of decayed plants and natural materials that enrich soil
    c. The cost of a postage stamp

15. Ozone layer
    a. Upper atmosphere
    b. Little people who lived in the land of Oz
    c. How much money is owed

16. Pollinators
    a. People who survey the public to find out people's opinions or how they'll vote
    b. Insect or creature that moves pollen from male to female plants
    c. Medicine for people allergic to bees and pollen

17. Biofuel
    a. Energy source made from living plants
    b. Purchasing gas
    c. Powering something with your own energy, such as pedaling a bicycle

18. Hybrids
    a. Something powered in more than one way, such as with gas and with electricity
    b. Waving at birds
    c. Measuring how high birds fly

19. Biodegradable
    a. A grade in biology or science
    b. Capable of being broken down (decomposed) naturally
    c. A science degree

20. E-waste
    a. Everyday garbage
    b. Discarded electronics, such as computers or cell phones
    c. Energy waste

Be an Earth BFF

Answer Key

1. c; 2. b; 3. a; 4. c; 5. c; 6. b; 7. a; 8. b; 9. b; 10. c; 11. c; 12. c; 13. b; 14. b; 15. a; 16. b; 17. a; 18. a; 19. b; 20. b

Scoring

Give yourself one point for each question you answered correctly, than add up your score.

15–20 The Queen of Green

Girl, you are a go-green machine! Whether you've been at this awhile or you're just jumping into the green scene, you are gung-ho when it comes to helping the world be a better place. Happy trail-blazing, but be sure that while you're brushing up on your eco-facts and stats that you're also taking plenty of time to actually *enjoy* God's beautiful earth. Picnic baskets, not picket signs!

10–14 Nature Lovin' Green Gal

You go, girl! You're becoming a better friend to the earth every moment. You already have some green sense and are well on the path to continuing your green-minded ways. You love and appreciate all things related to nature, so now it's time to become more conscious about your actions. Dig into more facts and activities to get even greener. Next time you head out on a nature hike, for example, take along a bag for snagging stray trash along the trail.

5–9 Go Green Team Player

Congratulations! You've gotten off the bench and gotten into the game of going green. You're well on your way to helping the earth and God's critters. But instead of always just following the pack, strive to be mindful on your own. You can grow even greener by making regular habits of recycling and energy saving activities you practice at times. It's easy to make going green a personal habit. Maybe you could even become a lead player by, say, kicking off an eco-friendly project at your school or church.

0–4 New-to-the-Scene Green Machine

You're a toe-tipper in getting your feet in the dirt, but you're reading this book so clearly you're ready to do your part in helping the earth. Becoming green doesn't have to be scary or mean you gotta get dirt under your fingernails. Get in the green habit with simple actions like flipping off switches when you leave a room and carrying a cute canvas bag when you shop. Discover the fun of a green spa day and yummy green cuisine, then team up with girlfriends to head outdoors and make the world greener!

Eco-Careers

Down to Earth

- **Material Removal Worker**

  "I clean up harmful waste."

- **Environmental Scientist**

  "I study problems that hurt the earth to find solutions."

- **Meteorologist**

  "God controls the weather, and I try to predict it."

- **Nuclear Power Engineer**

  "I design ways to get electricity from splitting apart little tiny atoms."

Caring for God's Critters

Got a pet you love? Maybe it's a fluffy fur-ball of a feline or a squiggly-wiggly goldfish. It's fun to play fetch with a dog, watch a guinea pig run through a maze, or see how other critters move, eat, and play. But the animals that you keep as household pets are only a few of the amazing creatures God made. He also created small fluttery butterflies, huge humpback whales, and chatty climbing monkeys and thousands of other critters that fascinate us … and need our care and respect.

Many of these creatures even help us, like horses that carry people and cows that give us milk. Discover how we can learn from animals in Proverbs 30:24–31. Be a nature friend to your pets and other animals by making the land around your home cozy, inviting, and safe. Or grow a plant that attracts butterflies or hummingbirds. God wants us to care for *all* the creatures he made …

"Those who do what is right take good care of their animals."

Proverbs 12:10

Be Kind to Animals

Do what you can to help God's creatures and eco-systems. Whether or not you own a pet, here are some things you can do for our furry and feathered friends:

- **Leave water outside** in a shallow dish for thirsty critters, since animals need water more than food to survive. Use warm water in winter.

- **Put out nesting materials for birds**, such as animal fur, yarn, or dried grass.

- **Put bells on** cat and dog collars as a warning for birds and small animals.

- **Leave an area uncut** in your yard so it grows naturally with weeds, woods, tall grass, or wild flowers for animal habitats.

- **Leave an old log** or tree stump in your yard for animals to build homes.

- **Plant berry patches** for animals to eat.

- **Clean boots** before hiking in new areas to remove any non-native seeds.

- **Plant native plants** to restore native ecosystems.

- **Use natural and organic** pesticides and insect repellents.

- **Make dog gifts,** such as homemade treats and toys, for a local animal shelter. Oh, yeah, and your pet will love them too! How-to instructions below:

Whole-Wheat Doggie Treats

When donating these dog biscuits, be sure to pass them on to an appropriate staffer at the animal shelter. Don't just go in and feed the dogs, since many of them are on special or restricted diets. This recipe makes two types of treats.

What you need:

1 cup whole-wheat flour
½ cup cornmeal
1 teaspoon baking powder
½ cup cheese
Crumbled bacon
1 teaspoon olive oil
⅔ cup liquid (water or chicken stock that has no onion)
½ cup peanut butter

What to do:

1. Mix the flour, cornmeal, and baking powder in a bowl.
2. Divide the flour mix in half into the two bowls.
3. To one half, add the cheese, crumbled bacon, olive oil, and ⅓ cup of the liquid.
4. To the other half, add the peanut butter and remaining liquid.
5. Roll out dough, and cut into 1-inch-by–3-inch strips. Fold over ends of each strip and press with fingers to form ends of dog-bone shape.
6. Place treats on ungreased cookie sheet. Bake at 325 degrees for 20 to 30 minutes. If harder biscuits are desired, turn off heat at end of cooking and leave treats in oven to harden.

Fido, Fetch! Roll Over, Rover ...

Make some simple toys for dogs to help the animal shelter cut down on costs.

What you need:

Scraps of rope
Polar fleece fabric
Scissors

What to do:

Knotted Toy

1. Cut rope 6–10 inches, depending on the dog's size.
2. Make a large knot in the center of the rope.

Knotted Dog Blanket

1. Cut two squares of polar fleece, each the same size. Cut square larger than the dog's body when the dog is lying down.
2. Cut off a 3-inch square from each corner.
3. Fringe the edges, 3-inches deep and 2 inches apart.
4. Use matching fringe pieces from each piece and tie them in a knot.

Game! Animal Signs Scavenger Hunt

This kind of hunting is all in good fun— and no animals get hurt in the process. Get some friends together for a scavenger hunt in which you take photos instead of picking up and collecting items as you find them.

Here's how to play:

1. Divide players into teams of two, and give each team a digital camera and a list of items to hunt down.

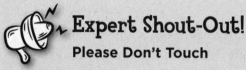

Expert Shout-Out!

Please Don't Touch

When your pet needs medical attention, you take it to the vet. But what should you do if you come across a wounded animal or bird in the wild? Follow these safety tips from a camp director and naturalist:

- **Don't try to touch** the animal. Even if an animal that isn't hurt comes near you, hands off! Nature is not a petting zoo.

- **Call an animal rescue** facility, and have them take care of the animal.

- **If you need to take emergency precautions**, first get an adult to help, then make sure everyone wears gloves to help prevent the possible spreading of disease. An emergency would only be if the animal is in danger of getting more injured before help could arrive, such as if the injured animal is on a road. Try to get the animal contained, and then get it to an animal rescue facility.

Identify animals around your home. Mark a circle of ground. Study the area in the circle for several days, and try to recognize what creatures left prints or other signs.

2. Set a time and place to meet back up, and then take off with your teammate to go look for the items (recommended scavenger list, below).

3. When you see an item on the list, snap a pic!

4. At the appointed time, meet back up to share photos and see which team found the most items on the list.

Scavenger list:

Worm, bird, feather, flying insect, leaf, berry, nut, seed, cat, dog, crawling bug, tree where animals live, hole in ground, animal track, wild mammal or rodent, lizard, grass, dirt, rock, outdoor water source. (Change or add to the list, depending on the creatures where you live.)

Out here in the country there are animals all over. I feel happy to see wild birds because they are free and happy and they should stay free.

— LEAH D., AGE 10, FLORIDA

Turf and Surf ...

There are two main types of ecosystems that provide homes for living creatures:

1. **Terrestrial** ecosystems are on land and include forests, deserts, grasslands, and mountains.

2. **Aquatic** ecosystems are water-based and include rivers, ponds, and lakes (called freshwater ecosystems), and oceans (called marine ecosystems).

"Praise the Lord from the earth, you great sea creatures and all ocean depths, lightning and hail, snow and clouds, stormy winds that do his bidding, you mountains and all hills, fruit trees and all cedars, wild animals and all cattle, small creatures and flying birds, kings of the earth and all nations, you princes and all rulers on earth, young men and women, old men and children."

PSALM 148:7–12

Weird but True! Amazing Animal Facts

- **Frogs are predators.** They eat other creatures, mainly insects, and live on land and in water. When the environment changes, frogs respond first, so they are known as an indicator species.

- **Brrr ... butterflies don't like the cold.** Antarctica is the only continent where the winged beauties have not been found.

- **Dogs shaking their bodies** to dry off inspired the invention of more efficient washing machines, dryers, and other appliances that use spin cycles.

- **There are a million ants** for every human on earth. That means we are far from being the most populous species—we're way outnumbered!

- **Goldfish need light** to keep their color. Without enough sunshine, their colors fade away.

- **Dolphins sleep with one eye open** and one eye closed. Only half of their brain is asleep at a time, while the other half stays awake. Gives a whole new meaning to the term "half asleep," huh?

- **Snails can sleep for up to three years** at a time!

- **A blue whale's tongue weighs more** than most elephants. Yes, that's just the tongue.

- **Bats always turn left** when exiting a cave. Going cave-dwelling? Enter with caution ... from the right side.

- **Hummingbirds can fly backward**—they're the only creatures that can complete such a feat. Pretty tricky!

- **Octopi have no bones** and are very flexible. They can squeeze through holes just slightly larger than their eyeball.

- **Dog nose prints are unique** to each animal and can be used to identify them, just as human fingerprints uniquely identify us.

- **Houseflies hum constantly** in the key of F. Who knew they were so musically inclined?

- **Sharks lay the largest eggs** in the world.

- **Humpback whales are the loudest** creatures in the world. They can be heard up to 500 miles away from where they are located.

- **All polar bears are left-handed.**

- **The snub-nosed monkey sneezes** when it rains. That's why this recently discovered monkey is called, duh, the *sneezing monkey*.

✨ *Real Girl* ✨

Sweet Reef Retreat

Emma, age 12, attended a summer retreat camp, where she helped to make an artificial reef ball. Emma says, "Making the reef ball was fun because you got dirty and knew you were helping out animals." She explains how it was made: First, they built a wire cage and placed balls into the wire. Next, they mixed concrete and poured it over the cage. After the concrete dried, they pulled the balls out so that the reef would have room for fish and coral creatures that will use it as a home. Then, a boat towed the reef way out in the ocean. The reef Emma made measured about two and a half feet around. Over the years, real coral attaches to the ball to create a new reef for other animals to live in.

Why Make a Reef Ball?

Coral reefs are made up of both plants and animals and are home to twenty-five percent of all marine life. Warming waters, pollution, and overfishing have caused the death of some coral reefs. The amazing thing is that we can help the coral using manmade materials. Reef balls are made using a concrete that can survive over 500 years and sustain itself through ocean waves. When these reef balls are placed into the water and populated with coral they can have a reef that will look and act as natural as the ones God created … and in just 3 to 5 years. It takes decades for a coral reef the size of a reef ball to form. So this is one way to help marine life recreate a natural environment.

Quiz

Hope for Endangered Animals

Each of the animals listed here was once endangered. Not anymore! See if you can match each animal with the reason for its removal from the endangered-species list.

1. Brown pelican
2. Gray whale
3. American alligator
4. Grizzly bear
5. American peregrine falcon
6. Whooping crane
7. Aleutian Canada goose
8. California condor
9. Idaho springsnail
10. Pine Barrens tree frog

a. Trade of animal hides was prohibited

b. Scientists found a significant population of these animals

c. Relearned migratory patterns by following ultralight aircraft

d. The animal was found to be the same as another species which is common in other areas

e. Use of endrin (a pesticide) decreased

f. Conservation of their habitat and outlawing their hunting

g. Once they were bred in captivity, the animal handlers wore costumes so these animals would bond with their own kind. The animals were then successfully reintroduced to the wild.

h. Hunting of these animals was prohibited

i. The Environmental Protection Agency (EPA) outlawed the use of DDT

j. Foxes were removed from its habitat

Answer Key:

1. e; 2. h; 3. a; 4. f; 5. i; 6. c; 7. j; 8. g; 9. d; 10. b

Eco-Careers

Animal Kingdom

- **Camp Caretaker**

  "I keep the campgrounds animal friendly and safe, and develop programs to help campers enjoy the wildlife."

- **Wildlife Biologist**

  "I make sure animal habitats are considered before workers mine, cut lumber, or start new recreation programs in an area."

- **Animal Rescue Worker**

  "I care for hurt and abandoned animals. I feed, water, bathe, and groom them."

- **Veterinarian**

  "As an animal doctor, I help keep pets healthy and treat them when they're sick or hurt."

chapter 5

Wet and Wonderful Water

Boom! Oops. Oil and gas exploded into a huge fireball. It caused one of the biggest problems in the ocean *ever*. It's called the Deepwater Horizon oil spill. Men drilling for oil made a mistake and caused a leak. Scientists expected it to take years to clean the mess the spill caused in the Gulf of Mexico.

However, something amazing happened. A long time ago, God created special bacteria that eat oil. The bacteria, especially a kind called Colwellia, gobbled up the oil and gas. There was so much oil that the bacteria had to multiply really fast just to keep up. Fifty-two kinds of bacteria and microbes helped clean the Gulf.

Plus, thousands of people volunteered to help— although, only trained people with safety equipment and experience to wash oil off ducks and other wildlife could actually pitch in. The ocean and shore have been getting cleaned up much faster than expected. People *can* make a difference!

"Who is a God like you, who pardons sin and forgives the transgression of the remnant of his inheritance? You do not stay angry forever but delight to show mercy. You will again have compassion on us; you will tread our sins underfoot and hurl all our iniquities into the depths of the sea."

MICAH 7:18–19

Oil and Water Don't Mix!

Oil is a detrimental pollutant to water. Every year, people pour 363 million gallons of oil down drains! That oil seeps into oceans, rivers, and lakes. Be sure your family disposes of oil from your car safely by putting it in a closed container and bringing it to a recycling center that collects used oil. Most cars hold about five quarts. You can check your driveway where your car gets parked to see if it is leaking oil.

Almost half of oil that spills into the ocean all around the world comes from natural leaks. Every year about 41 million gallons of oil leak into the Gulf of Mexico naturally. There's lots of oil under the ground below the ocean. Many leaks are from cracks in the earth at the bottom of the sea where the oil then flows out, floats to the surface of the water, and spreads out into thin layers. Microbes are drawn to these natural spills to eat the oil. Whales and fish then swim after the microbes to eat them, so the natural leaks are part of the marine life food chain. Satellites map the natural oil leaks—one of the largest is near Santa Barbara, California.

It's important to stop pollution, and to keep everything clean, healthy, and safe.

— Skylar, age 10, Florida

Oil Spill Cleanup Experiment

Investigate ways to clean up oil spills with hair and other materials.

What you need

2 T. of cooking or motor oil
Water
Container
Feather
A lump of hair from a hairbrush, disposable diapers, any other materials you think will remove the oil

What to do

1. Pour water into the container.
2. Add oil and watch it float on the surface. Notice that oil doesn't blend with water.
3. Dip the feather in the oily part of the water and then pull it out. Feel the slick oil on the feather? That's what coats birds and other animals.
4. Try to lift the oil off the water's surface with the hair and other materials to see which ones work best. Materials that absorb and remove oil are called sorbents.

There's a way to clean oil spills twice as fast as ever before, thanks to a contest that inspired companies to find new and better ways to remove oil from water. Team Elastec/American Marine won the contest by inventing equipment that removes 4,670 gallons of oil per minute. It's good to invent new ways to clean up pollution!

Beach Debris Cleanup

Every year volunteers clean up beaches and pick up hundreds of tons of waste. Items pulled out included balloons tied together, a refrigerator, car engines, cigarette butts, soda cans, and even toilet seats. Help clean up a beach or park in your area.

Evaporation = Desalination

Did you know that seventy percent of Saudi Arabia's drinking water comes from making salt water drinkable? Taking the salt out of water is called desalination. Try removing salt from water with the following experiment where evaporation purifies the water. Evaporation is when water changes to vapor and rises in the air.

How to Purify Water

What you need

Small container
Large bowl
Water
Dirt
Plastic wrap
Tape

What to do

1. Mix a cup of water and a spoonful of salt or dirt in the bowl, to make salty or polluted water.
2. Put the small, empty container in the center of the bowl with the opening facing up.
3. Cover the opening of the larger container with plastic wrap and tape it down.
4. Put the container where sunlight will hit it during daytime.
5. Wait about a week and look in the container. You should find clean water in the small container.

Huh . . . How Did That Happen?

Wondering how clean water ended up in the small container? The heat of the sun causes the water to evaporate. Over time the water collects on the inside to the plastic wrap. This is called condensation. The evaporated water begins to condense at the top of the container (just like the water condenses in the clouds). When enough water has collected under the plastic it gets heavy and will "rain" into the small container. The salt or dirt does not evaporate, but remains in the bowl. This is how sun cleans water naturally.

✨ Real Girl ✨

Taking a (Lemonade) Stand!

Brynnan, age 11, learned about the need for clean drinking water in Africa, so she and her BFF Mazie brainstormed ways to help. They came up with a Drink Up fundraiser to raise money to build wells. They  decided they could afford to buy inexpensive drinks, then sell them at a price increase to raise money for the organization. Drinks help remind people of thirst and the need for clean water. They sold drinks to their fifth-grade class and at a sports event. Now they're planning and organizing events for their entire school and church.

I thought helping my church raise money for wells was really good because of the muddy water they would have to drink and maybe get sick and die. These wells would give them clean water. It makes me feel good to help other people.

—EMMA, AGE 9, WEST VIRGINIA

All is Well . . .

You simply turn on the faucet and get clean water, but that's not true in all countries. In other parts of the world people don't have toilets, so when they go to the bathroom it goes into rivers and lakes and causes pollution that makes the water undrinkable. These poor countries don't have the money to build systems to clean the water. In other countries they don't get enough rain for water to drink. In some places people cut many trees to build homes and burn for heat and cooking. The lack of trees caused droughts (no rain). Some countries have so many people they don't have enough water for everyone. Many people in this world suffer because they don't have enough clean water. *Challenge yourself*: Think of ways to raise money for wells for clean water . . . and do it! Every little bit helps.

Be a Water Detective

Try these simple ways to detect water waste:

- **Shower with the drain plugged** to see how much water you use.

- **Brush teeth with drain plugged** to see how much water you use.

- **Stop, look, and listen for drips** from each faucet in your home. Check outdoor water spigots too.

- **Check showerheads** to detect leaks. If the water shower-head fills a one-gallon bucket in less than twenty seconds, you're wasting water. Ask an adult to help you replace the showerhead with a model that is more efficient.

- **Drop green food coloring** in your toilet tank. If the water turns green in the toilet bowl when you have not flushed the toilet, you have a leak.

Easy Ways to Conserve Water

Here are some simple good habits to pick up that will save you tons of water in the long run:

- **Store a pitcher** in your fridge instead of running water until it's cold.

- **Use a pan of water** to wash fruits and veggies instead of holding them under running water.

- **Buy clothes** that can be easily washed instead of ones that need dry cleaning that uses chemicals that can pollute.

- **Sweep the driveway** and sidewalk instead of hosing it down.

- **Collect water** used for rinsing fruits and vegetables to water houseplants.

- **Collect water** from your roof as it runs down the gutter and use it to water your garden.

- **Soak pots and pans** instead of letting the water run while you scrape them clean.

- **To cool off,** use a sprinkler in an area where the lawn needs to be watered.

- **Place dropped ice cubes** in a container with a houseplant instead of tossing them in the sink.

- **Place ice cubes** under the moss or dirt of hanging baskets, planters, and pots to give your plants a cool drink of water. This also prevents water from overflowing.

> **No Longer Dammed** In 1928, men made a dam so they could build a highway across southern Florida. The dam blocked water from flowing into the Everglades National Park. This hurt many plants and animals. The Everglades lost more than half its birds that wade in water. Now workers replaced parts of the road with a bridge and broke the dam. Hooray! The water, called the River of Grass, is flowing again.

- **Keep a bucket** in the shower to catch water as it warms up or runs. Use this water to flush toilets or water plants.

- **Don't panic** over cloudy water. Air bubbles cause water to look cloudy.

- **Flush dog and cat poop** down the toilet. It contains bacteria and other contaminants that go into the ground and get washed into waterways.

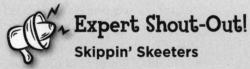

Expert Shout-Out!
Skippin' Skeeters

A scientist who works in the Florida Everglades explains that pesky mosquitoes produce in areas with standing water. It's recommended that you protect yourself from mosquitos naturally, without using harsh chemicals that irritate skin and can pollute the environment. Try citronella grass, marigolds, rosemary, catnip, and mosquito plants, or use a bug jacket.

Quiz

Can You Guess the Gallons?

Match the numbers with the facts. Note that the amounts are averages.

a. 100 gallons of water

b. 70 gallons of water

c. 150 gallon of water

d. 4 gallons of water

e. 23 gallons of water

f. 15 gallons of water

g. 2 gallons of water per minute

h. 200 gallons of water

i. 500 gallons of water per year

j. 97

k. 39,090 gallons

l. 2 gallons

m. Two-thirds

Answer Key

1. e; 2. f; 3. d; 4. a;
5. b; 6. g; 7. c; 8. h;
9. i; 10. l; 11. j; 12. k;
13. m

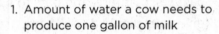

1. Amount of water a cow needs to produce one gallon of milk

2. Amount of water used by a standard washing machine

3. Average amount of water that flows out of a faucet per minute

4. Water savings monthly if shower is shortened by 2 minutes

5. Average water used by each person in America each day

6. Amount of water to fill an average bathtub

7. Amount of water used by a newer energy-efficient washing machine

8. Fixing a leaky toilet can save this much water every day

9. Water wasted with a showerhead or faucet that drips 10 drops per minute

10. Amount of water used to manufacture one new car

11. Amount of water that flows from an average faucet in one minute

12. Percentage of water on earth that is salt water

13. Percentage of US streams too polluted for fishing

Eco-Careers

Water World

- **Customer Service Representative**

  "I help customers understand their water bill and help with water quality concerns."

- **Laboratory Technician**

  "I test water for quality and germs, and report what I find."

- **Waste Water Facility Manager**

  "I check the water and plan for water usage. I also try to figure out how weather will affect the water."

- **Marine Biologist**

  "I study animals that live in and near the water."

- **Oil Spill Responder**

  "I examine areas hurt by oil spills and determine ways to safely clean up the spill."

Let's Clear the Air

Air is all around you even if you can't see it, so take a deep breath and think about what it is you're inhaling. Fresh air supplies the body with oxygen, which does all kinds of wonderful things. Oxygen strengthens the immune system, helps children grow faster, improves a person's heart rate and blood pressure, and even alters the level of a natural brain chemical called serotonin— the happy hormone!

Air also collects dust, smoke, and tiny particles of pollutants. Dirty air can cause burning eyes, itchy throats, and even breathing problems. Not good for a nature girl who likes fresh air! Your city or town might even have air alerts of days when you need to stay inside because the pollution is too high. That can be an epic problem on days you planned to play sports or picnic with friends. But, when the air is clean, it's time to celebrate in the great outdoors.

Switch up activities to focus on nature, such as planning outdoor fun instead of hanging out at the mall. Grab friends and plan nature outings, attend outdoor concerts, and even enjoy campouts. Get outside, fill your lungs with fresh air, and discover natural beauty that's more gorgeous than store bought bling.

> *"The spirit of God has made me, and the breath of the Almighty gives me life."*
>
> Job 33:4

What's the Dirt on Air Pollution?

If you're puzzled about air pollution, just think of how smoke can make you cough and how fog makes it hard to see. Small particles in the air from factories, cars, and even spray cans cause what is known as smog. That's a type of man-made fog that fills the air with particles we don't want to breathe in. Air quality measures pollutant particles and lets people know if it is safe to be outdoors. Weather forecasts often include reports on air quality.

Air pollution isn't new. One of the plagues in Egypt is related to pollution when Moses tossed ashes in the air and it hurt people's skin.

> *"So they took soot from a furnace and stood before Pharaoh. Moses tossed it into the air, and festering boils broke out on people and animals."*
>
> Exodus 9:10

The good news is we can team up with God to clean the air.

Be an Air Detective

We can't capture gases in the air, but we can capture particles.

What you need:

Petroleum jelly
Index cards
Masking tape
Microscope or magnifying glass

What to do:

1. Smear petroleum jelly on an index card.
2. Tape the card outside, on a fence or side of the house, and leave it for a few hours.
3. Remove card, and look at it with a magnifying glass or microscope to see particles on it. It might look like dust, or maybe an insect or carbon particles.
4. See if you can identify the particles. Some might be dirt blowing, while other particles are pollutants. (You'll see more if you look at the cards under a microscope, if you have one.)
5. Try placing cards in several locations, and note differences. Check to see if rain cleans the air by putting out cards before and then after rainfall.

Oh-So-Fab Air Freshener

Looks pretty and refreshes the air! What's not to love? Lasts about a month, as it disappears into the air.

What you need:

¾ cup hot water
1 envelope unflavored gelatin
1 tsp. salt
4–5 drops essential oil
4–5 drops food coloring
Baby food jar
Lacy fabric scrap
Hair elastic

What to do:

1. Mix very hot water (you can boil it) with the gelatin and salt.
2. Add in 4 – 5 drops each of essential oil and food coloring.
3. Mix until gelatin dissolves.
4. Pour into baby food jar, and let sit overnight until it gels.
5. Cover top of jar with fabric, and secure with hair elastic. Add a ribbon to make a pretty gift.

Zesty Citrus Spritz

This air freshener is for girls who love to squirt!

What you need:

Citrus fruit
Grater
Pan of water
Spray bottle

Grate outer peel off any citrus fruit (also called the zest) and boil in water. Let cool completely, then drain and discard the peels, and pour the water into a spray bottle. Spritz it everywhere needed (in vacuum cleaner bags, garbage disposal, waste baskets — yes, even your stinky  shoes!). Experiment with adding spices, such as cinnamon sticks, to the hot water, or fresh herbs like basil or sage.

What in the World is the Greenhouse Effect?

Think about hopping in a car on a hot day after the car sat in the sun with the windows closed. The car trapped air inside and it heated up like a greenhouse for tropical plants. Ugh! You're not a tropical plant and it's too hot to sit inside until you open the windows and let the air cool.

This same thing happens in our atmosphere that happens in the closed car. Some of the gases and excess carbon dioxide that pollute our air trap heat in the earth's atmosphere. Many scientists believe that could be causing weather changes around the world. This theory is called the greenhouse effect. You can be part of the solution by not using spray cans with aerosols that give off gases that trap the air and by using less fossil fuel energy that gives off carbon dioxide.

"For the Lord himself will come down from heaven, with a loud command, with the voice of the archangel and with the trumpet call of God, and the dead in Christ will rise first. After that, we who are still alive and are left will be caught up together with them in the clouds to meet the Lord in the air. And so we will be with the Lord forever."
1 THESSALONIANS 4:16–17

Fresh air is important so you can breathe and so you can dance through life.
— AINSLEY L., AGE 9, GEORGIA

Tree-mendous Air Fresheners

Trees are God's cleaning and cooling machines. Leaves suck in air, including chemicals, and then moves those chemicals to the roots. Tiny creatures that live in a tree's root system change the chemicals into food. Trees breathe out clean oxygen we need to breathe. Plants help too, but trees are much bigger and do the cleanup faster. Plants become great helpers at cleaning air indoors (it's hard to grow a tree inside a house). Trees can't clean up all the air, so we also need to change our habits that add gases to the earth.

Plants to Purify Indoor Air

Plants can be amazing roommates. They help create more oxygen while removing pollution and toxins from the air around you. To top it off they never complain about what you're doing or even if you room is a mess (although, they'll droop if you forget to water them). Here are just a few recommended houseplants and the great help they can be in your home. Ask your parents about getting one to take care of and help your home freshen up a bit.

- **Spider plants** are great for removing xylene, a chemical found in rubber gloves and printing inks.

- **Snake plants** are great in bathrooms to reduce humidity and filter out formalde-hyde that is found in cleaning products, toilet paper, and personal care products.

- **Chrysanthemums** are great for hanging in a window as they need direct sunlight. They filter out benzene found in glues, paints, plastics, and detergents.

- **Golden pothos** is a great plant for the garage. It can stay green even in the dark, and it will filter out the formaldehyde from car exhaust.

- **Azaleas** improve the condition of air in a basement, if you can find a bright spot. They do best in cool areas and combat formaldehyde as well. They remove chemicals found in floor-cleaning products.

- **Aloe vera** and **philodendrons** also filter out formaldehyde.

Houseplants Need Lotsa Love!

Before getting a plant consider the care it needs:
- Most houseplants prefer semi-dark areas, but can adapt to average or indirect sunlight.
- Plants need soil that's damp but not too wet.
- Dust leaves with a damp sponge to keep them healthy and breathing well.
- Hydroponic plants grow in water filled with nutrients instead of rooting in soil. Sometimes, they have clay pellets or coconut fibers in the pot they grow in for support, but they get their food from special water. One great thing about a hydroponic plant is you never have to weed it. Since roots take chemicals out of the air, a hydroponic plant is more purifying than a regular plant.

Daniel and the King's Dream

"These are the visions I saw while lying in bed: I looked, and there before me stood a tree in the middle of the land. Its height was enormous. The tree grew large and strong and its top touched the sky; it was visible to the ends of the earth. Its leaves were beautiful, its fruits abundant, and on it was food for all. Under it the wild animals found shelter, and the birds lived in its branches; from it every creature was fed."

vợć ấâđꞡNꞏсB Kʋꞈb

Daniel listened to King Nebuchadnezzar describe the first part of a vision from God. This part used the image of a healthy and beautiful tree to picture the king. A healthy tree provides shelter and homes for creatures, and grows large, with juicy fruit. It's a wonderful picture of how as nature girls we can have fruitful lives and care for all God made. The ending of the vision was not so good as it warned the king that if he made bad choices he would lose his position and the ability to help others and the earth.

Be a Tree Detective

Take a walk or hike, and really pay attention to the trees around you.

- **Tree rings are like pages** of a tree's personal scrapbook. Each ring shows one year of the tree's growth. Find a stump and count the rings to see the tree's age. Wider rings show a year with more rain and growth. There may be scars that show a fire.

- **Listen to trees breathe** by using a glass or stethoscope. The sap in tree moves similarly to blood in our veins and arteries.

- **Look for clay** around a tree's base, and remove it with a shovel. A tree can be smothered if people dig and toss clay around it. Clay keeps air from getting to the roots, so the tree dies.

> **Don't hold your breath to save the earth. Plant a tree instead.** One young tree absorbs thirteen pounds of carbon dioxide (CO_2) a year by breathing it in. People breathe out CO_2, a little over two pounds each day. Burning fossil fuels releases CO_2. A car produces about twenty pounds a year. There needs to be a balance between carbon dioxide made and used. With more cars, houses, and cutting trees down we get out of balance and then there's too much CO_2 in the air that can add to the greenhouse effect. CO_2 is what makes the fizzy bubbles in soda, so we need to be careful how much fizz we add to the air.

- **Loosen compressed dirt**. Large machines that drive over tree roots and press dirt tight can also smother trees. If dirt is too compacted, break it up some with a garden tool.

- **Check the roots** of trees around your house. If roots are on the surface without much soil, add some mulch, which contains nutrients and won't smother the roots. Mulch is any type of covering put around plants to help keep the water in the soil. Examples are grass clippings, straw, compost, and broken pieces of bark.

- **Look up at the top** of the tree. This is the canopy. The roots go out as far as the canopy, so water that far out to be sure you're getting to the roots.

Without trees we wouldn't have fresh air.

— MEGAN, 11, CALIFORNIA

Expert Shout-Out!

Cut That Out ...

A climate control specialist shared these details: A person in Africa with no electricity cuts a tree to cook food, heat water, and keep warm. The person might not think to plant a new tree or even have money to buy seeds to plant. Three billion people cook and heat with wood because they don't have electricity, and that means they chop down many trees, which is causing problems in tropical rainforests. It's a complicated problem that hurts our air.

What's up with chopping trees to cook? It might not sound bad, but when a tree is cut the carbon dioxide it stored is released into the air. Deforestation actually added more to air pollution in the past decade than all the gas given off by vehicles. The fumes the wood fires give off also adds to pollution. When too many people chop trees and don't replace them fast enough it causes changes in the ecosystem. Trees attract clouds and that means rain. Without trees, a drought starts and the land turns to dust. That dirt blows around and also adds to pollution.

So to stop the cutting of trees in Africa we have to solve the reason they cut the trees down and that's lack of electric power. We need to do it with ways that don't hurt the environment or cost a lot of money.

Africa is working to solve the problem:

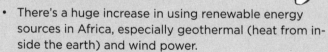

- They are investing in solar power in many of the countries in Africa.

- In Kenya people use millions of small solar powered lanterns for light.

- There's a huge increase in using renewable energy sources in Africa, especially geothermal (heat from inside the earth) and wind power.

- People are replanting trees in Africa, particularly where leaders understand the problem and allow the planting.

Quiz

Name These Trees, Please!

God knows how important trees are to clean air. He created some awesome trees, and you can find many types of trees named in the Bible. Unscramble the name of each type of tree in this list. The Bible verse where they are mentioned is beside the scrambled word.

1. igf   __ __ __   Genesis 3:7

2. aaicca   __ __ __ __ __ __   Joel 3:18

3. kao   __ __ __   Judges 6:11

4. eloiv   __ __ __ __ __   Psalm 128:3

5. mpla   __ __ __ __   Exodus 15:27

6. plpea   __ __ __ __ __   Song of Songs 8:5

7. kmarista   __ __ __ __ __ __ __ __   Genesis 21:33

8. wwlloi   __ __ __ __ __ __   Ezekiel 17:5

9. riuft   __ __ __ __ __   Leviticus 19:23

10. oarplp   __ __ __ __ __ __   Hosea 4:13

11. sloea   __ __ __ __ __   Psalm 45:8

12. reulmbry   __ __ __ __ __ __ __ __   Luke 17:6

13. eipn   __ __ __ __   Ezekiel 27:6

14. file   __ __ __ __   Proverbs 3:18

15. mdanol   __ __ __ __ __ __   Jeremiah 1:11

16. ursypc   __ __ __ __ __ __   Isaiah 44:14

17. oaeycrsm   __ __ __ __ __ __ __ __   Luke 19:4

18. emoprganate   __ __ __ __ __ __ __ __ __ __ __   Deuteronomy 8:8

19. draec   __ __ __ __ __   Ezekiel 31:3

20. yetmlrs   __ __ __ __ __ __ __   Isaiah 41:19

Answers

1. "Then both of them knew things they had never known before. They realized they were naked. So they sewed **fig** leaves together and made clothes for themselves." Genesis 3:7

2. "At that time fresh wine will drip from the mountains. Milk will flow down from the hills. Water will run through all of Judah's valleys. A fountain will flow out of my temple. It will water the places where **acacia** trees grow." Joel 3:18

3. "The angel of the Lord came. He sat down under an **oak** tree in Ophrah. The tree belonged to Joash. He was from the family line of Abiezer. Gideon was threshing wheat in a winepress at Ophrah. He was the son of Joash. Gideon was threshing in a winepress to hide the wheat from the Midianites." Judges 6:11

4. "As a vine bears a lot of fruit, so your wife will have many children by you. They will sit around your table like young **olive** trees." Psalm 128:3

5. "The people came to Elim. It had 12 springs and 70 **palm** trees. They camped there near the water." Exodus 15:27

6. "'Who is this woman coming up from the desert? She's leaning on the one who loves her.' The woman says to the king, 'Under the **apple** tree I woke you up. That's where your mother became pregnant with you. She went into labor, and you were born there.'" Song of Songs 8:5

7. "Abraham planted a **tamarisk** tree in Beersheba. There he worshiped the Lord, the God who lives forever." Genesis 21:33

8. "Then it got a seed from your land. It put it in rich soil near plenty of water. It planted the seed like a **willow** tree." Ezekiel 17:5

9. "When you enter the land, suppose you plant a **fruit** tree. Then do not eat its fruit for the first three years. The fruit is not clean." Leviticus 19:23

10. "They will spring up like grass in a meadow. They will grow like **poplar** trees near flowing streams." Isaiah 44:4

11. "Myrrh and **aloes** and cassia make all of your robes smell good. In palaces decorated with ivory the music played on stringed instruments makes you glad." Psalm 45:8

12. "He replied, 'Suppose you have faith as small as a mustard seed. Then you can say to this **mulberry** tree, "Be pulled up. Be planted in the sea." And it will obey you.'" Luke 17:6

13. "They cut all of your lumber from **pine** trees on Mount Hermon. They used a cedar tree from Lebanon to make a mast for you." Ezekiel 27:5

14. "She is a **tree of life** to those who hold her close. Those who hold on to her will be blessed." Proverbs 3:18

15. "A message came to me from the Lord. He asked me, 'What do you see, Jeremiah?' 'The branch of an **almond** tree,' I replied." Jeremiah 1:11

16. "He cuts down a cedar tree. Or perhaps he takes a **cypress** or an oak tree. It might be a tree that grew in the forest. Or it might be a pine tree he planted. And the rain made it grow." Isaiah 44:14

17. "So he ran ahead and climbed a **sycamore**-fig tree. He wanted to see Jesus, who was coming that way." Luke 19:4.

18. "It has wheat, barley, vines, fig trees, **pomegranates**, olive oil and honey." Deuteronomy 8:8.

19. "Think about what happened to Assyria. Once it was like a **cedar** tree in Lebanon. It had beautiful branches that provided shade for the forest. It grew very high. Its top was above all of the leaves." Ezekiel 31:3

20. "They brought a report to the angel of the Lord. He was standing among the **myrtle** trees. They said to him, 'We have gone all through the earth. We've found the whole world enjoying peace and rest.'" Zechariah 1:11

Eco-Careers

Air Quality

- **Air Quality Associate**

  "I check emissions from cars and factories, evaluate air pollution sources, and check air quality."

- **Air Quality Engineer**

  "I calculate emissions, interpret laws about the air, and analyze how pure the air is and how much pollution is in it."

- **Forester**

  "I plan the use of forests and renewing forests. I make reports about land a company wants to buy and their plans and reasons to want the land. I also check on how many trees are in a forest."

- **Landscape Architect**

  "I design outdoor areas for homes, parks, buildings, and factories."

Power Up!

Powering up a computer, charging a cell phone, or spinning an MP3 player are daily activities for many gals. It can be a challenge when the power goes off. *What?* No heat or a/c, no microwave, and no power to recharge electronics? Thankfully, God created all we need to harness power. He made fossil fuels we burn and turn into electricity. God is creative and also made renewable energy sources. Renewable energy means it is always available or easily regrown. Nuclear energy is not a fossil fuel, but it's not renewable either.

What difference does it make as long as you can plug in a favorite game or turn on a great DVD? Lots, so get in the know. Burning fossil fuels produces pollution, and nuclear energy can be dangerous and produces contaminated byproducts. Renewable energy is safer, but it costs much more. Scientists and engineers keep working on cheaper ways to harness renewable energy. A nature girl makes choices to use energy wisely and wants to use renewable energy when possible.

"Command the people of Israel to bring you clear oil that is made from pressed olives. Use it to keep the lamps burning and giving light all the time."

Leviticus 24:2

Be Wise on How to Energize!

Turn on a switch, plug something in to a socket, or use a battery. That's using electricity. But what is it really? It's energy that comes from electrons moving around. You probably can understand it's easier to run through air than pudding, and that's true for electricity too. Electricity is more easily made when electrons move through certain materials called conductors. Electricity is made from grabbing the energy from natural resources like water, the sun, or a burning lump of coal. Here are the various resources we use to make energy:

- **Solar Energy** Sunshine is free! But turning it into energy can be expensive. Large rectangles made of silicon are called solar panels. They lie in the sun—usually on rooftops—collect heat, and change it into electricity.

- **Wind Energy** Wind, like sunshine, is a gift from God. And it, too, costs some money to harness. Besides, wind is uncontrollable—who even knows when it will blow or where? So it must be combined with other power sources for backup. Windmills, called turbines, convert wind to energy.

- **Nuclear Power** Nuclear energy comes from an element called uranium and a process where an atom is split. Sure, it's affordable. But radioactive remains and nuclear waste must be safely controlled. Microbes have been found that eat the waste, so that helps! The U.S. is starting to build newer and safer nuclear power plants.

- **Oil** It's a natural resource and reasonably affordable. So what's the prob? Pollution. There are ways to get oil from a type of rock called shale, and there's plenty of it in America.

- **Hydropower** Water provides one-fifth of the world's energy. It's not from drinking it, but from letting it flow. As water runs downhill it can spin a wheel to generate power. However, manmade dams built to make water run downhill can destroy wildlife habitats and ecosystems, so that means we need to make wise choices.

- **Natural Gas** It has no smell and burns easily. Plus, it's very plentiful and cleaner than other fossil fuels. People worry about the carbon emissions and possible leaks. A smelly substance is added so people can detect leaks.

- **Coal** It's cheaper than oil or gas but creates more pollutants, like sulfur dioxide (chemical that causes acid rain) and small particles. New technology captures the particles to use for sheet rock and other building supplies. Coal generates nearly half of the world's energy.

- **Biofuels** Squeeze olives or crush peanuts and you'll get a slimy liquid. Such oils from plants that can be used for fuel are called biofuels. Growing plants for fuel uses space needed to grow food for people and making more land to grow biofuels can harm habitats. The easiest biofuels to use are used cooking oil.

- **Gasoline** Gas comes from refining crude oil, also called petroleum. The crude oil is also used to make many other products like plastics, crayons, and even nail polish.

Sneaky Ways to Save Energy

These ideas for saving energy are so simple they'll become second nature:

- **Unplug chargers** once your gear is fully charged.

- **Buy rechargeable** batteries for electronics you use.

- **Turn off lights** and appliances when you leave a room.

- **Wash clothes in cold** or warm water instead of hot.

- **Hang clothes** up on a line to dry them.

- **Choose Energy Star** electronics, such as TVs and computers.

- **Adjust thermostats** in your home—even 1 degree makes a diff!

- **Ride your bike** or take a hike instead of hitting the mall or movies.

- **Use a solar flashlight** instead of battery-operated.

- **Be ready** to try new things. Someday your shoes could power your cell phone or MP3 player. Scientists are working on methods to capture the energy heat released when people walk.

"He gives strength to the weary and increases the power of the weak. Even youths grow tired and weary, and young men stumble and fall; but those who hope in the Lord will renew their strength. They will soar on wings like eagles; they will run and not grow weary, they will walk and not be faint."

Isaiah 40:29–31

Be an Energy Detective

There are at least three ways to discover air leaks of hot or cold air escaping your home. Such leaks cost money for the energy used to heat or cool your home. Try some of them, then help your parents plug leaks.

- **Flashlight Test.** At night when it's dark, turn the lights off in a room, and be sure all windows and doors are shut tight. Have one person stand inside the room and shine a flashlight along the edges of windows and exterior doors, while another person stands outside and notes any light that passes through. Wherever light escapes, so does air.

- **The Paper Method.** Close a window or exterior door on a slip of paper. See if you can pull it out easily. If so, there's a leak.

- **Hand Method.** On a cold day when you have the heat on to keep warm, use your hand to test for leaks. Just place your open hand around the edges of your windows and doors inside. If you can feel cold air on your hand, you've found a leak.

Easy Breezy! In closed-up spaces where the air doesn't flow, stale air can build up. Stale air can cause dizziness, nausea, headaches, and even anxiety and grouchy feelings. On nice days, open windows to let fresh air inside. *Bonus:* It saves on heating and air conditioning. And, well, it just smells better and feels great to let the sun shine in!

"And God said, 'Let there be light,' and there was light. God saw that the light was good, and he separated the light from the darkness."

GENESIS 1:3–4

We need to think of a way to conserve fossil fuels because it takes too long to make them. And poof! One day we will run out and there goes our transportation.

—HANNAH, AGE 9, OHIO

Fun-in-the-Sun Fashion Police

Who says you can't wear white in winter? Well, do what you will but there *is* some fashion sense behind this classic style rule. Your clothes capture heat from the sun, so check out how your wardrobe choices make a difference on hot or cold days.

What you need:

White T-shirt
Black T-shirt
2 ice cubes

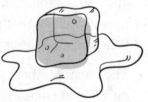

What to do:

1. Place both T-shirts on the ground in a sunny area on a warm day.
2. Put an ice cube on each of the shirts.
3. Watch to see which ice cube melts faster.
4. The color of shirt that causes the ice cube to melt first, is the one that absorbs more light and heat. When you wear it, it'll keep you warmer as it takes on heat.
5. The shirt with the slower-melting ice cube reflects light and will keep you cooler on a warm day.

Solar Blast with Glass!

The first solar scientists used glass to increase solar energy. You too can see how it works …

What you need:

2 ice cubes
One clear drinking glass
One tinted drinking glass

What to do:

1. Place both ice cubes on the ground outside on a sunny day.
2. Put the clear glass upside down so it encases one of the ice cubes; put the colored glass over the other ice cube.
3. Watch to see which cube melts first.

How it works:

Clear glass acts as a conductor and insulator of the solar energy. Air will be warmer under the clear glass, so the ice will melt faster. This is why sitting in a house by a sunlit window is often warmer than sitting outside in the sun.

Sunlight in a Jar

Use the rechargeable light part of outdoor lights to convert jars and clear plastic containers into small indoor lamps. These can be decorated and covered to diffuse the light for pretty indoor solar lighting. Such lights change the sun's energy into electricity with the use of a non-metallic element called selenium.

What you need:

Outdoor solar light (can be found at many stores, including dollar stores)
Heavy-duty double-sided clear tape or adhesive putty
Empty clear plastic or glass containers with clear lids

(continued)

Outer covering material:
    Organza or other see-through fabric (find some with
        pretty patterns or sparkles)
    Vellum paper sold with scrapbook papers
    Lace with a very open pattern
    Non-woven tissue paper that is eco-friendly and feels
        like fabric
Rubber bands

What to do:

1. Unscrew the lid from the solar light. Use the lid that includes the battery, solar panel, and light bulb for the top.
2. Use adhesive to attach the top with the solar panel against the inside of the lid of the clear container. Put the lid on the container.
3. Cover the container. Wrap the fabric or paper around the jar and stick it with the adhesive. Use a rubber band to hold the top in place under the lid.
4. Set jars in windows to recharge during the day. If needed, turn jar on its side to get sunlight on the solar panel.

Add creativity

- Cut shapes out of the vellum paper or fabric, such as stars or hearts to create stencils.
- Try filling the stencil openings with a contrasting color covering fabric.
- Add a ribbon over the rubber band for decoration.
- Use translucent paint or markers to color the jar.

Game! Light the Way

In ancient times, Egyptians used sunlight and mirrors to light paths in tunnels. Play a game using your solar-light jars (how-to-make, see above).

What you need

Solar light jar
Mirrors, one for each player
A target object

1. One person will start with the solar light, and everyone else will hold mirrors.

2. Stand in two lines, about three feet apart.

3. The person holding the light (in the front of one line) should angle it in such a way that it hits the mirror of the person at the front of the other line.

4. The person holding the mirror now moves his or her mirror so the light reflects off the mirror and hits the mirror of the second person in the opposite line.

5. Continue passing the light down the lines, using reflection until the last person shines the light on the target.

6. Try changing locations.

7. Once you can do this easily, spread the group out and around corners to see how far you can move apart and reflect the light.

Get Creative! Make up your own games, such as a pass-the-light variation of musical chairs.

Solar energy is everywhere. I watched my little brother make a solar-powered microwave at science camp. I also watched my papa install a solar panel to heat his pool. We used solar-powered lights when we went camping.

— HANNAH, AGE 9, OHIO

Easy Lovin' Solar Oven

Yep, use the sun's heat to cook snacks for you and your friends! Here's how to make your very own easy-cook solar oven.

What you need:

Pizza box (or similar box with folding lid)
Aluminum foil
Tape
2 wooden, or metal, skewers
Black construction paper
Round metal pan
Clear glass pie pan or lid

What to do:

1. Line the inside of the pizza box (including lid area) with aluminum foil, shiny side facing up. Tape the foil at the beginning and end of the lining.
2. Use skewers to hold box open at an angle (a little less than the lid being straight up). Figure out where to place the skewers to hold the box at this angle, then poke tiny holes in the cardboard to put the ends of the skewers in to keep the box open.
3. Add aluminum foil to the sides of the box. Pull off a sheet and attach it to the back and bottom of the box allowing the skewers to help hold up the long side of the foil. This will increase the solar energy taken in by your box.
4. Place a piece of black paper into the bottom of the box. You will be placing your foil pan on top of this with your food in it.

How to use your solar oven:

1. Bring your solar oven outside and turn it toward the sun for cooking. It will cook best at the hottest and brightest part of the day, between 11 a.m. and 2 p.m. Place it on a high enough surface that any animals around your home will not be able to reach it, but low enough that you can check your food.
2. Make sure the day is not windy or your cooker might blow over. If you place it so your house blocks the wind, make sure the cooker will stay in the sun for the entire cooking time.
3. Place the food in the pan and into the cooker. Cover the food with upside-down clear glass pie plate or glass lid for faster cooking (the recipe times that follow use the glass cover).

Some simple solar recipes... When you are removing the food from the solar cooker, it might be hot, so handle it with care by using hot pads or tongs to remove the pan from the cooker, and then let it cool a little before eating.

Sunny-Side-Up Cheese Sammie

Cooking time: 40 minutes

What you need:

Butter
Sliced bread
Sliced tomato
Sliced cheese

What to do:

1. Butter a piece of bread, and put it into the pan, butter side up. Follow solar oven cooking instructions, above.
2. Add a slice of tomato, and top with cheese. Cook until the cheese is melted. For crispier bread, put a buttered slice in for about 15 minutes before adding toppings.

Sun-Smooched S'mores

Cooking time: 1 hour, 15 minutes

What you need:

Graham crackers
Chocolate bars
Marshmallows

What to do:

1. For each S'more, place half a graham cracker in the pan. You can cook a few at a time.
2. Add a piece of chocolate on top, then top with a marshmallow.
3. Once the marshmallow and chocolate melt, add the other half of the graham cracker to finish the S'more. If you want your marshmallow a little crispy, before cooking squish it between your fingers just a bit until it gets some cracks—the sun makes the cracked areas crispier.

Recycle! If you and your friends are drinking soda with your sun-kissed snacks, be sure to toss the cans in a recycling bin. One recycled can saves enough energy to power a TV for three hours. Why? The can, even if you crush it, is already made of aluminum, and that's the key ingredient to make a can. Turning raw materials into aluminum means digging bauxite out of the earth, turning it into aluminum, and then making a new can. Whew! That takes more work, which means using more fuel.

✨ *Real Girl* ✨

Growing Up (gulp) With No Electricity

April grew up in a rural area of South Florida in a house not connected to power lines. Her family used propane tanks to power the stove and refrigerator, but they had no electricity to switch on lights. April never felt deprived living without air-conditioning or artificial lighting. She learned to enjoy the outdoors. April says the hardest thing about not having electricity was keeping up with overall cleanliness: "We had to heat water on the stove for baths and sweep the rugs instead of vacuuming." When she was about fifteen, April's family had electricity hooked up. But April still rarely uses air-conditioning, and prefers candle-light to harsh light bulbs and lamps.

Caution: Only use candles with permission and after an adult explains how to safely use them. Container candles are the safest.

Quiz

Test Your Energy Smarts

Check off the choices you make and what you know about energy to see how savvy you are when it comes to conserving resources.

1. When you buy a new electronic gadget, you...
   a. Look for the one with the most sparkles
   b. Check the star performance
   c. Go for the cheapest

2. What saves more energy when preparing meals?
   a. Oven
   b. Microwave
   c. Serving raw food

3. What costs more in terms of energy—a computer or Xbox?
   a. Xbox
   b. They use about the same amount of power
   c. Computer

4. What uses more energy—a shower or bath?
   a. Bath
   b. It's about the same
   c. Shower

5. When you are the last to leave a room, you...
   a. Always turn off lights and electronics
   b. Sometimes turn things off
   c. Try to remember to turn stuff off, unless your brother turned it on!

6. When you go shopping, you…
    a. Always ask for paper bags
    b. Always ask for plastic bags
    c. Bring your own reusable canvas bag

7. Star appliance means
    a. It sparkles
    b. A government label that shows it is energy efficient
    c. Safety tested and reliable

8. In case the power goes out, you have…
    a. Candles and matches
    b. Solar-powered lights
    c. Rechargeable flashlights

9. When it comes to using batteries, you…
    a. Buy cheap ones but recycle them
    b. Avoid buying anything that uses batteries
    c. Recharge

10. When you get your homework back, you…
    a. Crumple it up and toss it
    b. Use the flip side, then recycle
    c. Throw it right away into the recycling bin

Scoring

Questions 1–5: Score 3 points for every a answer, 2 for every b answer, and 1 for every c answer

Question 6: Score 3 points for a or b answers, and 1 point for each c answer

Questions 7–10: Score 1 point for every a answer, 3 for every b answer, and 2 for every c answer

10–16 Points: Energetic Techling

You're a techie girl who likes her gadgets and enjoys using energy. Next time you plug in your headphones, perhaps it would do you some good to listen to an inspirational talk on energy conservation. OK, boring! But seriously, be more conscious of how much energy you're sucking up.

17–23 Points: Savvy Energy Saver

Yeah, yeah, you know the drill… Turn out the lights, unplug appliances, walk or bike to the store. It appears you try to save energy when you can, but why not take a few more steps to be even *more* conscious of your choices? It's great the you're so eco-smart, but bump it up a notch when it comes to your energy-saving endeavors.

24–30 Points: Super Power Tripper

Wow! Not only do you save energy at every turn, but you're constantly tapping in and staying tuned to new developments in energy conservation—as well as being creative when it comes to your own use of energy. Now that's what we call girl power!

Eco-Careers
Energy Resources

- **Reliability Engineer**

  "I plan and figure out what we need to keep equipment running well. I try to bring in newer equipment that saves energy."

- **Senior Solar PV Installer**

  "I add solar panels to homes and businesses."

- **Residential Field Engineer**

  "I help bring other types of energy into homes, like wind and solar power. I also get the permits and inspect the work."

- **Electronic auto engineer**

  "I create and build hybrid and electric vehicles."

chapter 8

Real Girls Reuse and Recycle

When you go shopping and get to the checkout counter, store clerks often ask how you prefer to have your purchases packaged: "Paper or plastic?" So ... what's a girl to do? Paper is made from trees, while plastic is made from petroleum oil. Some people think paper is better because it returns to dirt faster. Others point out that making and recycling paper uses almost twice the energy, water, and resources compared to making and recycling plastic.

Of course, you could always carry your own reusable cloth bag when shopping. Still, the issue doesn't stop there—what about the stuff that's *in* that shopping bag? Are you making conscious decisions when it comes to being a consumer, or do you mindlessly toss stuff into your shopping cart? Choices are not always easy, so do your research and think about the purchases you make. Challenging yourself to scope out the items that are kind to our earth makes shopping way more fun! So *think* before you buy, use, or toss things out …

> *"The simple believe anything, but the prudent give thought to their steps."*
>
> PROVERBS 14:15

Be a Brainy Buyer

Instead of shopping on a whim … ask yourself a few things first:

- **"Why do I want to purchase this item?"** Do you *love* it or *need* it? If not, it's likely a wasteful splurge.
- **"How was this item manufactured?"** Did an earth-friendly company make it? Does it contain organic ingredients or components?
- **"How does the use of this item impact the earth?"** Was it made using things that can decompose easily? Is it made using efficient energy? Does this item do a better job taking care of the earth than other similar items? Does it use less packaging than similar items?
- **"Can this item be recycled or repurposed?"** What will happen to this when I finish using it? Can I pass it onto a friend? Can it be made into something new?
- **"Where will the packaging and other waste go?"** Biodegradable means the product can break down and return to a natural form safely. Everything biodegrades over time, but natural products given to us by God break down much more quickly.

How Degrading!

Find out how long it takes different items to biodegrade (break down or decompose).

What you need:

Spade or other tool for digging
Items to test (examples: cucumber slices, Styrofoam cup, paper towel, plastic bag)

What to do:

1. Bury the items in an outside area that gets sun.
2. Draw a map of where you buried each item, and mark each spot with a Popsicle stick.
3. A month later, dig up the items. Note which items disappeared into the soil and became part of the dirt again. Those are biodegradable items. Tiny creatures (microorganisms) and worms help break items down. God created such creatures to help renew the earth.
4. Look at the items that didn't change or break down into the soil. They could take years to biodegrade. Or they may remain unchanged for centuries, like ancient pottery archeologists dig up.

How Long Does it Take for Items to Return to Dirt?

Some items decompose and become dirt again quickly. Others? Not so much. Check out this list to see how long different items take to break down. Plastic is new, so scientists don't really know how long different types will take to decompose. Scientists have done tests to make estimates that are in this list:

- Paper towels: 2–4 weeks

- Paper: 2–5 months

- Apple core: 2 months

- Paper: 1–3 months
- Cardboard box: 2 months
- Wax-coated milk carton: 3 months
- Cotton T-shirt: 6 months
- Wool sock: 1–5 years
- Banana peel: up to 2 years
- Cigarette butt: 1–5 years
- Plastic bags: 10–20 years
- Leather boot: up to 50 years
- Rubber sole (of the boot): 50–80 years
- Tin soup can: 50 years
- Plastic bottle: 100 years
- Aluminum soda can: up to 200 years
- Plastic six-pack rings: 400 years
- Disposable diaper: 450 years
- Fishing line: 600 years
- Plastic drink holder: 1 million years
- Styrofoam cup: indefinite
- Glass bottle: 1 million years

The Three R's

There are three key actions you can take to help cut down on waste:

Reduce: The first step is to *reduce* the amount of energy you use and buy fewer things.

Reuse: The next step is to *reuse* as much as you can. Archeologists dig up ruins that are centuries old, and they often find pottery and glass. Because these items have not biodegraded, they are great for re-use.

Recycle: The last step is to *recycle* what is waste (what you decide to throw out). *Recycling* depends on having places that accept waste for recycling and ways to remake the items into something new. It only takes two months to make a soda can into a new can and place it back on a store shelf. Some materials can only be recycled for so long. For example, after paper fibers have been recycled four to five times, they become too weak to be recycled again. Finer paper can be recycled up to a dozen times. Aluminum and glass can be recycled forever.

Bonus Round!

Here are a few more R's to keep in mind when it comes to loving the environment:

Repurposing: To use an item in a new way. For example, after emptying a can of corn you can use the can to hold pencils.

Renewable Resources: Energy sources that are replenished so there's no limit to the supply, like sunshine, wind, and water. Put out solar lights that get recharged by the sun. Bamboo is more than food for Pandas. It's a great, renewable resource. Bamboo plants grow up to four feet a day, take in large amounts of CO_2, removes nitrogen to help prevent water pollution, and don't need pesticides or much care. Bamboo is 100-percent biodegradable. Bamboo is being used for making floors, furniture, wooden spoons, and even fabric.

Respect: This means to value and honor. You respect the earth when you pick up liter to keep it clean, renew a plot of land, or walk without disturbing plants and habitats.

Paper that Makes a Difference!

If you saved some of your early schoolwork you may notice the papers are starting to fade, tear, and look old. Acid in the paper causes it to lose color and break down. Acidic foods like vinegar taste sour. Well, acid in paper makes the paper get sour. But there's good news because you can buy acid-free paper and it's also better for the environment. Trees that are used to make paper are naturally acidic and so the pulp has to get special treatment in order to become acid-free. Most scrapbooking and art paper is acid-free because the paper keeps its color and won't get brittle. The water used to make acid-free paper gives off less corrosive chemicals so the water can easily be reused. It's super earth-friendly. The paper is easier to recycle and can be recycled many more times than regular paper. Such paper in landfills does not give off harmful acids into the ground. It's even good for the paper company. The machinery to make the paper lasts longer too since they use less chemicals that corrode machinery.

The Resourceful Potter

"I did as he told me and found the potter working at his wheel. But the jar he was making did not turn out as he had hoped, so he crushed it into a lump of clay again and started over. Then the LORD gave me this message: 'O Israel, can I not do to you as this potter has done to his clay? As the clay is in the potter's hand, so are you in my hand.'"
Jeremiah 18:3–6

God sent Jeremiah to watch the potter spin a wheel and turn a lump of clay into a jar. The jar didn't come out well so the potter crushed it and started again. He didn't toss out the pieces he broke. He reused the clay. Many times a potter will smash up a broken piece of pottery. That's called grog. Adding grog to soft clay will add strength and make it easier to form a good bowl, vase, or other beautiful work of art. Making something new out of what is broken is part of what recycling is all about.

God used the potter and clay to share how he works in our lives. When we think we have failed and feel broken inside God can use the broken parts of our life and make us new again. As you make new things from old with recycling crafts, remember to thank God for the recycling he does in your life.

Pretty Paper Project

Instead of tossing old homework papers into the recycling bin, use it to make pretty handcrafted paper!

What you need:

Scrap paper
Warm water
Medium-size bowl
Pair of hosiery ready to be discarded
Metal coat hanger
Large pan with sides
Flower petals

1. Tear scrap paper into 1-inch pieces. You need about 1.5 cups to make a sheet of paper.
2. Soak the scrap in warm water for 12 hours. You want to completely cover the paper and have about ¼ inch water in the bowl above the paper.
3. Blend the mixture until it looks like creamy soup.
4. Take the coat hanger and bend it so it is a square shape with a handle (most light coat hangers can be somewhat easily pulled out of shape—when you are finished making paper you can re-shape the coat hanger so it can be used in your closet again).
5. Starting at the part of the hanger without the handle, open the hosiery and pull it onto the hanger. It will end up with hosiery around the hanger making a screen with very thin holes.
6. Put the screen over a large pan with sides to catch excess water.
7. Pour the mixture through the screen, allowing the water to drain off.
8. Spread the solids out over the screen and add a few flower petals to the mixture.
9. Allow this to dry for at least 24 hours.
10. Peel off your new paper to use it.

Plastic Bottle Cap Necklaces

Turn plastic bottle caps into jewelry!

What you need:

Clean plastic bottle caps with flat tops
Scraps of aluminum foil
Tacky glue
Small beads or pebbles
Large bead
Jewelry chain, ribbon, or yarn

What to do:

1. Glue foil inside cap. You can cut it to fit inside the bottom of the cap or just rip a little scrap and lay it inside.
2. Fill cap with adhesive. Place tiny beads on glue in desired pattern.
3. Glue side of a bead to side of cap.
4. Slide a chain or ribbon through open ends of the bead to form a necklace.

Other Options:

- Use jewelry findings to make bottle cap earrings, key chains, or zipper pulls.
- Glue ribbon around side of bottle cap.
- Before adding glue and beads cover cap with a scrap of fabric (stretchy fabric works best).

Up-Cycling Can Games

Turn a can into a 3D game board, make magnetic pieces, and have fun. The pieces can store inside the can to make it an easy game on the go.

What you need:

Empty can and plastic lid
Paper scraps or colored plastic lids
Magnetic strips (check the fridge for old business cards
    and small calendars that have magnetic backing)
Glue
Permanent marker

What to do:

1. Cut strips to go around the outside of the can. These will form tracks. Add lines to make spaces for moving a player piece. Mark one end as the start. Color the spaces in a variety of colors. Glue onto can.
2. Make several playing pieces for each color. Cut plastic lids into small pieces that fit in the spaces of the strips made. Back each piece with a small piece of the magnetic strip.
3. Cut paper squares the colors used on the strips. Make a few of each color.
4. Draw a tic-tac-toe grid on the bottom of the can.

The Track Game

1. Drop the paper squares into the can. Each player places a game piece at the start for her track.

2. Take turns pulling out a colored square and moving the player piece to the next square of that color. See who gets to the finish first.

Tic-tac-toe

Each player needs 5 playing pieces. Play the tic-tac-toe on the bottom of the can.

Mix it up and make up new can games

Play the game but have each player find an object of the color in the room or in sight (could be a car color if playing in a car) within ten seconds in order to move.

Be creative and design your own games on other cans, such as one with ladders and slides, a round-the-can checkerboard, or one with green items on strips that must be spotted to move ahead.

Alphabet in All Caps

Make alphabet play caps to use with younger children. It's great if you have siblings or work as a mother's helper.

What you need:

26 plastic bottle caps
Permanent markers
Paper scraps
Glue

What to do:

1. Write one letter of the alphabet on top of each cap. You can color the cap a solid light color and then draw the letter in a dark color.
2. Draw 26 circles to fit inside the caps. You may find tracing a penny gives you just the right size and shape.
3. Draw a tiny picture for each letter. Try to draw green items like trees, apples, sun, or flowers.
4. Cut the circles and glue them into the matching lettered cap.

Using alpha caps

1. Use the caps to help children learn letters, sounds, and words that begin with the letter. Test skills by showing a picture and seeing if they know the beginning letter of the word.

2. Use caps to teach reading by helping children make words from a group of letters. You can even play scrabble!

3. Make a second set of alpha caps to play a matching game where you pull the caps out of a bag and try to get letters that match.

CD Jewelry

Make shiny earrings and necklaces with pieces of old CDs. They add sparkle and match everything!

What you need:

Used CDs
Nail file
Paper clips
Tacky glue

What to do:

1. Cut the CD into   shapes. To use all of the CD, cut rectangles by starting at the outer edge and cutting into the center hole. Cut pairs of triangles of the same size.
2. File any rough edges to make them smooth.
3. Glue a paper clip on the back of the jewelry shape.
4. String the pieces to make a necklace or link onto earring findings.

Optional:

Decorate the jewelry pieces. You can draw designs or

write names with permanent markers, or glue on beads.

More CD recycling fun

- Cut pieces of CDs and glue to a piece of cardboard to make a shimmery collage.
- Glue CD pieces to an old ball to make a disco ball.
- Hang several CD pieces from a cardboard circle to make a mobile. Hang it outside, and watch it reflect sunbeams.

Rad Ways to Recycle!

Since you can't turn *every* piece of trash into a craft project, here are some easy ways to reuse and recycle:

- **Place containers** in your bedroom near your waste-basket for recycle materials. Have fun with it by decorating used boxes, crates, or bins. Be creative— cover with fabric, color with markers, or design with decoupage.

- **Before you buy** a book, CD, or DVD, think about whether or not you want it in your permanent collection. Otherwise, you could rent, swap, or borrow one from a library or friend—or download!

- **When done with discs** you did buy, donate to a friend or library since they're made of a type of plastic that's difficult to recycle. Some discs are ground into small particles, like gravel, then used to make alarm boxes, jewel cases, automotive parts, and streetlights. A number of office supply chains and places that sell music and movies have started collecting and recycling them, so check local stores.

- **Take used supplies**, such as ink cartridges and electronics, to office-supply stores that help with recycling. Check your local office stores and recycling centers to find out what they take. Many have special e-cycling days for electronics.

- **Used cell phones and small electronics** can often be recycled through services at your local post office. You can look online for a list of which ones recycle or ask your local postmaster.

- **Have a swap party** with your BFFs, or plan a swap session at your church. Have people bring clothes, toys, games, anything they want to pass on. Group like items together, then "shop" to your heart's content—for free! What's left can be donated to a charitable organization.

- **Use both sides** of paper and then recycle it. It takes 60 percent less energy to make new paper from old than making it from trees. One ton of paper = seventeen trees. Save paper by using a lunch box instead of using paper bags or make a fabric scrap one (see Chapter 7).

- **Collect, clean, crush**, and turn aluminum cans into cash. One pound of aluminum = thirty-one average-sized cans. So at approximately forty cents per pound, you can earn about a dollar for every eighty cans you collect. Americans toss out lots of soda cans—enough to rebuild all our commercial airplanes!

We buy a lot of things from thrift stores and Ebay and sometimes Craigslist. I use plastic containers to make

piggy banks and other stuff.

— ELIZABETH, AGE 9, KANSAS

The Never Ending Fabric Trail

Goodwill, Smart Association, and other non-profit organizations make it easy to recycle items made from fabric. At one time everything had to look like new or gently worn. Now all clothing is green unless it has oil or hazardous chemical stains! Good clothes are resold or sent to people in poor countries. Here are some ways fabric is recycled:

- Some fabric is used to make industrial cleaning wipes.
- Stuffed animals become the stuffing in car seats.
- Old sweaters make good carpet padding and filling for softballs.
- Old clothes are also shredded apart for the fibers and then woven into new cloth.
- Fibers from jeans are used to make insulation for houses.
- Leftover fabric scraps become paper money.
- Shoe soles become paving material so you might be driving over your old shoe soles!

Gather up your old stuffed toy, even if an ear or other part is missing, clothes, and anything made from fabric (even carpets), wash it, and donate it. It doesn't matter where you take items for recycling since charity groups pass on what they can't sell or use to the recycling industry.

Expert Shout-out!

Fashion Trendy Actions

The executive director of Secondary Materials and Recycled Textiles Association (SMART) says,

"Everyone can make the earth a greener place by recycling the clothes they no longer wear, want, or need. Stop your clothes from ending up in a landfill and give them a second chance at making someone else feel great about how they look. Remember, nearly 100 percent of all clothing, shoes, and other textiles can be recycled. If you wear it, you can recycle it."

"When they had all had enough to eat, he said to his disciples, 'Gather the pieces that are left over. Let nothing be wasted.'"

JOHN 6:12

Real Girl

The Snacker Generation

Morgan, age 12, and her Girl Scout troop made reusable Velcro snack bags as a part of their bronze award project. They made bags with washable fabric and Velcro closures. They made the bags to help the environment, as people using these would use less plastic and create less trash.

They began by researching the best material to use for the bags and then learned to sew so they could make the bags. They created over 200 bags and sold them to family, friends, and at a band concert. With the money raised they bought toys and art supplies for a local pediatric unit and emergency room.

DIY Reusable Bags

Make your own fabric bags from scraps and then use them to hold snacks, game pieces, jewelry, and other small items.

What you need:

2 pieces fabric (one should be waterproof, like nylon from a broken umbrella or old windbreaker)
Velcro
Thread

What to do:

1. Cut two pieces of fabric into matching squares or rectangles. Place the fabric right sides together.
2. Sew three sides of fabric pieces together. Turn the fabrics right side out.
3. Turn down the open edges. This will be the top of the bag.
4. Cut Velcro the length of the top of the bag.
5. Sew one side of the Velcro to the top of the bag.
6. Sew the other side of Velcro to the bottom of the bag.
7. Fold the bag in half so Velcro closes. Sew sides closed.

Quiz

Trash-to-Treasure Match-up

What do recycled products become? Match each recycled product with the new item it becomes.

Recycled Item

1. Newspaper
2. Magazines
3. Cereal boxes
4. Cardboard
5. Notebook paper
6. Metal cans
7. Aluminum cans
8. Glass
9. Plastic bottle #1
10. Plastic bottle #2

New Item

a. Toilet paper
b. Bike and car parts
c. Plastic lumber
d. Paper bags
e. Paper backing on shingles
f. Telephone books
g. New jars and bottles
h. Fleece jackets
i. Aluminum cans
j. Countertops

Answer Key

1. j) Newspaper = Countertops
2. f) Magazines = Telephone books
3. e) Cereal boxes = Paper backing on shingles
4. d) Cardboard = Paper bags
5. a) Notebook paper = Toilet paper
6. b) Metal cans = Bike and car parts
7. i) Aluminum cans = Aluminum cans
8. g) Glass = New jars and bottles
9. h) Plastic bottle #1 = Fleece jackets
10. c) Plastic bottle #2 = Plastic lumber

Eco-Careers

Reuse and Recycle

- **Second Hand Store Owner**

  "I own a store that allows people to share items no longer needed with others."

- **Recycling Center Worker**

  "I take recyclables and break them down so they can be made into new materials."

- **Recycling Artist**

  "I create art from used items — recycling someone else's garbage into beautiful new creations."

Party at the Park

Parks are great for enjoying the outdoors. They are places to hang out, picnic, play ball, run, watch wildlife, hike, sit to enjoy nature, and be prayerful. In America we are blessed to have many types of parks. National parks are of interest to all citizens because of the geology (unusual land formations) or history (such as battlefields). Some are huge and others are small areas with monuments. There's at least one national park in every state so check out the one nearest your home! State parks are special to people because of the historical significance or preservation of natural beauty and allowing everyone to enjoy areas, such as beaches. Local parks provide recreational areas for area residents. Some communities even have neighborhood parks and playgrounds. Think of all the places to party at and celebrate the land!

We want to protect all our parks and other land areas for people to enjoy and for animals to have homes, and that's called conservation. We can care for the dirt, the critters, the buildings (we need bathrooms too), and the plants. Parks need care to keep the soil healthy and to remain a safe place to play!

National Park Paradise

Find out what national park is nearest your home. You can even take online tours of some at nationalparks.org. Here are some fun national park facts:

- **Our government created the National Park Service**. Yellowstone Park was the first in the United States. The most visited parks in America are the Great Smoky Mountains and the Grand Canyon.

- **Delaware, our first state, is the last state to get a national park.** The First State National Historic Park will be the 400th place in the national park system. It includes land called Woodlawn, along the Brandywine River, where President George Washington fought for our independence.

- **The Trail of Tears spans across nine states**, commemorating the journey traveled by foot, horse, wagon, and steamboat by Cherokee tribes that were forced to move from their homelands. This National Historical Trail includes land and water routes.

Check out your state parks too. Find out where they are located and why they are special.

> *"I made gardens and parks and planted all kinds of fruit trees in them. I made reservoirs to water groves of flourishing trees."*
>
> ECCLESIASTES 2:5 – 6

Bible Camp

A law in Georgia makes it a crime for groups to place a Bible in the cabins in their parks, but that could change. The governor wants the ban lifted since the state does not pay for the Bibles, and that would allow freedom of religion. Some people want to keep the Bibles out and say the state should not promote one religion. The governor points out that all groups are welcome to donate written materials.

Park It!

Add to the fun of going to a park by planning activities to do before you go.

- **Grab your ball**, Frisbee, or other sports equipment.

- **Pack a picnic** and invite your crush.

- **Put on your hiking boots** and follow or forge a trail.

- **Check with park rangers** to find out how and when you can volunteer at the park.

- **Have your family sign up** on a park email list to get notices of activities. Parks often offer special programs about animals, plants, or the night sky, or host free events like concerts, Easter egg hunts, guided hikes, or even outdoor movie screenings.

- **Take part in the recreation** at the park. They might offer boating, zip-lining, swimming, fishing, skeet shooting, or biking trails. Find out if there's a cost for any of the activities.

- **Bring a cool pen and notebook**, sit, and journal about all you see and hear.

- **Snap photos of scenic beauty**, fun with friends, and critters you spot.

- **Plan a challenge for your BFFs**, such as an orientation course or relay races.

- **Create a scavenger hunt** and leave a copy with the park ranger for other groups to use.

- **Plan a birthday party** or family reunion at a park.

- **Grab sunscreen**, towel, and friends, and rest and relax in the sun.

- **Enjoy a portable hobby** such as spool knitting, friendship bracelets, or making recycled crafts.

- **Stretch out on a blanket** in a beautiful setting and read a paperback or flip through a magazine.

- **Camp with your family** or youth group.

- **Bring a bird or plant guidebook** and identify the flying creatures or local fauna. Some park offices even print guides to plants and animals in the park.

- **Play hide-and-seek** if there are plenty of trees and areas where you can walk or run.

- **Bring some weather instruments** and record observations each season by checking the temperature, humidity, clouds, and wind speed.

- **Bring a telescope** for a park that's open after dusk and check out the night sky.

- **Ask permission to do soil tests** or plant native plants.

- **Walk your dog** at the park instead of around the block.

The USA has so much to offer and going to national parks is a great way to see all of it. Bring a camera!!! Also, good shoes because the big national parks have some awesome trails but they can get tough. In Summer 2011, we went to Olympic National Park in Washington State. And we played on a snowy mountain on the Fourth of July. That was surreal.

—Rebekah L, age 14, Florida

You're Invited: Park Party!

Plan a party at a park near your home. Everyone's invited to the shindig!

Invites

Grab a paper bag, cut it into 5-inch square sections, fold each section in half, and cut a half-tree shape on the fold. Color the top of the tree. Inside write the details (when, where, time, what to bring).

Eats

Tell guests to bring a food to share. Include plenty of water to stay hydrated. Consider these tasty treats:

- Fresh fruits
- Sandwiches or fixings for kids to create their own
- Trail mix (see recipe)
- Granola bars
- Chunks of cooked meat plus cut veggies and skewers to create raw kabobs
- Dips and pita chips

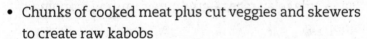

If you can cook on a grill, bring refrigerated rolls and hot dogs. Put the dogs on a stick or long skewer and wrap the dough around them and cook.

Decorations

Use natural items such as rocks and leaves to make arrangements.

Capture the Memories

Find special natural spots for photo shoots and take individual, BFF, and group shots at those places as well as pics with your crush. Also take photos of activities enjoyed at the party.

Fun

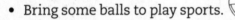

- Bring some balls to play sports.

- Plan a sing-along and ask any friends with guitars or other instruments to bring them. You can have everyone use sticks and tap in time to a tune.

- Have hula-hoops for contests or marking circles to observe nature close up.

- Make a list for a scavenger hunt (check Chapter 4 for one list).

- Bring binoculars to share and look up into tall trees.

- Plan some relay races—jumping, running, hopping, skipping.

- Bring your solar oven from Chapter 8 to cook treats.

- Make up an exercise trail. Plan a stop every few minutes or after walking a certain number of paces and then do an exercise such as jumping jacks, arm circles, squats, or hopping in place for thirty seconds.

- Bring a ball of yarn to use for trail blazing, make a volleyball net, or weave your own lacrosse sticks on forked sticks you find (if the park allows you to pick up sticks).

- Make sun tea in a clear plastic jar. Pour one cup water for each tea bag, add the tea bags, cover and let sit for two hours. Add sweetener and enjoy.

Enjoy the earth

Plan to sit, look, and listen to nature and then discuss what you noticed. Plan a prize for the friend with the longest list (maybe a new notebook for future observations or a small ball to remember to have fun).

Help the Park

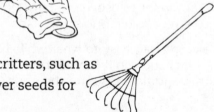

- Do a litter pick up.

- Bring food for park critters, such as berries and sunflower seeds for birds.

- Ask the park ranger ahead of time if there's a project you and your friends can help do and then bring any equipment needed (like shovels, rakes, or gloves).

- Take photos of your group enjoying the park and once you get home and print the pictures make posters on why the park is fun.

- Make a video about the park and all the fun it offers.

Spirit-Filled Trail Mix

Combine food snacks with spiritual food. A trail mix is loaded with possibilities, so feel free to substitute, add, or omit ingredients.

What you need:

2 cups whole-grain cereal puffs
1 cup almonds, any variety
¼ cup M&M's
2 cups small pretzels
¼ cup mini marshmallows
¼ cup sunflower seeds
¼ cup raisins or other dried fruit

What to do:

1. Put each ingredient in a separate bowl. (Tape ingredient tags on each bowl, with the info provided in the box on the next page.) Add a large spoon to the healthier foods, such as nuts and fruits, and small ones to the sugary foods like marshmallows and M&M's.
2. Let each person put a spoonful or more of ingredients they want to use into a bag. Make it greener by using the reusable fabric scrap bags from Chapter 8.

(Make the bag easy to wear while hiking. Sew O-rings on the sides and clip it to your belt or tie braid yarn to make a strap and tie ends onto the rings.)

Help Our National Parks!

Many parks are in trouble and don't have funds to fix problems. Most national parks have had at least one plant or animal species disappear, especially when non-native plants take over the land where native plants grew.

Sneezing and coughing? Oops! Many parks have air quality problems that make viewing the sites difficult, and make it hard to breathe.

Happy Trails!

Make tags for your trail-mix ingredient, using the following text, and tape to each bowl or on the table accordingly:

- **Cereal** is made from grain. Jesus told us he was like a kernel of wheat, in John 12:24: "Very truly I tell you, unless a kernel of wheat falls to the ground and dies, it remains only a single seed. But if it dies, it produces many seeds."
- **Almonds** remind us of Aaron's staff as a priest in Israel. "The next day Moses entered the tent. He looked at Aaron's staff. It stood for the tribe of Levi. Moses saw that it had not only begun to grow new shoots. It had also produced buds and flowers and almonds." (Numbers 17:8, NIrV)
- **M&M's** bring to mind a rainbow of colors, including red of Christ's shed blood, brown of the earth God made, green of growth, and yellow of light!
- **Pretzels**, shaped as arms folded in prayer, remind us God answers all our prayers and that Jesus prayed outdoors. "After leaving them, he went up on a mountainside to pray." (Mark 6:46)
- **Marshmallows** make us think of taking a softer approach to life: "A gentle answer turns away wrath, but a harsh word stirs up anger." (Proverbs 15:1)
- **Sunflower seeds** aren't mentioned specifically in the Bible, but seeds in general are referred to throughout and … from the very beginning: "Then God said, 'Let the land produce vegetation: seed-bearing plants and trees on the land that bear fruit with seed in it, according to their various kinds.' And it was so." (Genesis 1:11)
- **Raisins** represent the sweetness of falling in love in the poetry that is Song of Songs 2:5: "Strengthen me with raisins, refresh me with apples, for I am faint with love."

On the trail of life, God makes and keeps promises. He blesses along the way.

Building homes and businesses along the edge of parks sometimes hurts the land, and that hurts wildlife. Mining and drilling beside national parks can destroy wildlife habitats. Dams and other water usage for people can block the flow of water into a park. What does that have to do with you? Well, there are things you can do to contribute to the solutions and not the problems …

- **Pick up litter** you spot (yes, even if it's not yours!) and properly dispose of it. When visiting any park, leave things in as good—or better condition—as you found it.

- **Become a member** at a state or national park. The dues help fund that park, as well as provide programs to encourage others to enjoy the park.

- **Be a park friend.** National parks have a friend of the park group to join. They plan activities to help at the park.

- **Become a Junior Ranger** by learning more about a specific national park. Over 200 national parks offer a junior ranger program (go to nationalparks.org). You pick up a booklet of activities to do and then talk with a ranger afterward. You receive a junior ranger pin or patch once you complete the program.

- **Volunteer** to help out at a park. Once you are 15, you can be a part of the Youth Conservation Corps (npca.org) and help out with a variety of activities in a park. You can also check with the rangers at a local or state park and see if you can volunteer with a project now.

A Fish Tale

In Washington, D.C., and Maryland, four thousand students helped restore fish to the Chesapeake Bay and two rivers that flow into the bay. Students built hatcheries and raised fish in their classrooms. Three hundred thousand more shad are now splashing and swimming in the waterways thanks to the students. The program is called Schools in School Program.

Quiz

Name That Park Please!

Check out the clues and see how fast you and your friends can identify each National Park. This game covers fifteen national parks. Research and create clues for more parks to continue quizzing your friends.

1. Located east of the Mississippi
   Park includes mountains, woodlands, lakes, and ocean shorelines
   Originally named Lafayette National Park
   You can explore many miles of this park using the free Island Explorer Buses
   Name is an Algonquian Indian name that means "place of plenty"

2. It's the tallest mountaintop in the region
   Located in a northern, cold state
   Made of granite
   Known to be in the Black Hills
   People go to see carved faces of four presidents

3. Comprised of lakes, canyons, mountains, and rivers
   Located in the north and west in a large state
   It has a subalpine forest (freezing winters and cool summers)
   It was the first national park
   Most popular site of the Old Faithful geyser

4. It's an international biosphere reserve
   This park is in the Pacific Ocean
   Located on a big island
   Known for its volcanoes, including one active one, in our fiftieth state
   The most active volcano is Kilauea

5. Theodore Roosevelt expressed awe at the sight as he stood on the rim

   Includes 277 miles of river

   Located in the west in a state known for its deserts

   One of the natural wonders of the world

   Most famous for river gorge of the Colorado River

6. People visit to see the beautiful autumn colors

   The salamander capital of the world and home to black bears

   Near Cherokee, NC, home of the Cherokee

   Sixteen mountains of the Appalachian Mountain chain, including Thunderhead Mountain

   A natural fog hangs over these mountains, especially in the morning

7. Known for cold, snowy winters

   President Washington spent a winter here during the American Revolution (1777–78)

   Visit General George Washington's headquarters here

   It's near Philadelphia, where Valley Creek and the Schuylkill River meet

   On the first Saturday of each month from January to April, you can enlist in the Continental Army for a day of activities

8. Known for tall grass and wetlands

   In a warm state, it's the largest subtropical wilderness in the United States

   Ride an airboat here on the slow moving river of grass

   You can snorkel in this park

   Alligators live here

9. President Gerald Ford signed the bill to establish this park

   Visitors enjoy following the Towpath trail, a former path of the Erie Canal

   The park's name is Mohawk and means "Crooked River"

   There's a scenic train ride through the park

   Near Cleveland, it's the fifth most visited national park

Party at the Park

10. This park contains the largest protected area of Chihuahuan Desert in the United States
    Home to more than 56 species of reptiles in this large state
    Home to 450 species of birds
    There are more than 150 miles of trails to explore
    It borders the Rio Grande River and Mexico

11. Brr, this northern state experiences cold winters
    Visitors come by ferryboat
    The largest island in a great lake that's only 209 square miles
    75 percent of this park is underwater
    Known for its wolf and moose population that can cross on ice to Canada in the winter

12. Covers 531 square miles in this very cold state
    No roads lead to the park; access by ferries and air
    Travelers enjoy white water rafting plus spectacular sights of icebergs and glaciers
    Wildlife: black and grizzly bears, moose, wolves, salmon, sea lions, whales, bald eagles
    In the Yukon Territory, west of Juneau

13. Nicknamed the American Spa
    The smallest national park, and it's in a southern state
    There are mountains in the park
    Contains a famous collection of bath houses
    Very warm water comes from the springs here that are considered good for sick people

14. Pear Lake is here
    There are 275 caves at this location
    Along the Sierra Nevada Mountains, which includes canyons, mountains, lakes, and waterfalls
    Oldest tree in the park is thought to be 2,302,700 years old
    Known for its tall, gigantic red trees

15. There is no fee to visit any part of this park
    It is the home to many memorials
    It contains over 35 ornamental pools and fountains
    Located in our nation's capital
    Its tallest structure is 555 feet tall

Answer Key

1. Arcadia National Forest, Maine
2. Mount Rushmore National Memorial, North Dakota
3. Yellowstone National Park, Wyoming
4. Hawaii Volcanoes National Park, Big Island of Hawaii
5. Grand Canyon, Arizona
6. Smokey Mountains National Park, Tennessee
7. Valley Forge National Park, Pennsylvania
8. Everglades National Park, Florida
9. Cuyahoga National Park, Ohio
10. Big Bend, Texas
11. Royal Isle Park, Michigan
12. Glacier Bay National Park and Preserve, Alaska
13. Hot Springs National Park, Arkansas
14. Sequoia National Park, California
15. National Mall and Memorial Parks, Washington, D.C.

Eco-Careers

Park Services

- **Park Ranger**

  "I keep our parks safe and beautiful. I also plan programs to help visitors enjoy the park."

- **Wildland Firefighter**

  "I protect parks and forests from fires and fight them when they do happen. I even carry my own fire tent to protect myself."

- **Erosion Specialist**

  "I design plans to save soil. I work to control soil erosion."

- **Park Archeologist**

  "I study fossils found at parks and research exhibits to be sure we make them be true to real life and history of the area."

chapter 10

Sprouting a Green 'Tude

God created our precious earth, and we're his caretakers. We can be God's hands that care for plants and animals, and his feet that travel through its amazing wonders, and his mouth that shares both its beauty and the need to protect it with others. This book is about ways to respect and love all God made. And if we treat our planet and its inhabitants well, future boys and girls will also be able to appreciate the earth.

God's prophecies tell us that he has more plans. Scripture reminds us that God can renew the earth. You can partner with God in renewing the land, air, and water. Rock a green attitude each day by taking time to enjoy nature and switching up to greener habits.

Develop your critical thinking skills—those that help you examine issues and make wise choices. Find facts and read what scientists and volunteers are doing to help the earth, and look for solutions. Be sure to share your thanks to God with praises when you discover new wonders or see a beautiful sunset, flower, or natural scene. Share your love for the world God made and encourage others to live with a greener 'tude—one that screams, "I love this planet!"

> *"I am about to do something new. It is beginning to happen even now. Don't you see it coming? I am going to make a way for you to go through the desert. I will make streams of water in the dry and empty land."*
>
> Isaiah 43:19, NIrV

Simple Switch-Ups!

Here are some easy-breezy actions you can take that help develop attitudes and qualities that show you care about the earth and people:

- **Bring along a bag** for picking up litter when you take a walk. That's a green act of kindness.

- **Look and notice** something wonderful about a plant or creature to develop respect for the earth. Make this a daily habit!

- **Check electronics** and unplug after charging to be energy responsible. These energy vampires continue to drain power even when a device is fully charged. Consider getting a power charger that turns itself off with a built-in timer.

- **Study both sides** of an issue. Find out what studies have been done and what facts you can discover. This helps you have a balanced view.

- **Dig in and create** a beautiful garden for an elderly or disabled neighbor who needs help with lawn work. It's a great way to share your love of nature!

- **Learn to identify** all of the beautiful varieties in nature. When hiking a nature trail, pay attention to bird sounds, animal tracks, and types of trees and plants. This helps you appreciate nature!

Solution: No Problem!

It's a good idea not to ruminate when there's a problem, but at the same time, don't stick your head in the sand! Trusting in God is important, so look at a problem only long enough to see his perfect solution. Being courageous, which means being informed, is the first step to real change. When you hear about a problem with the earth, think things through with these steps:

- **Identify** the issue or topic.

- **List** what you know is true, both good and bad points, the advantages and the disadvantages. Underline the most important points of the issue.

- **Ask** questions you have about the issue.

- **Discover** resources to study the topic and answer your questions.

- **Find** out what studies have been done, who did the study, how they did it, and what they discovered.

- **Consider** possible future problems, such as "How long will the materials used for a project last and will they create more trash or be recyclable?"

- **Pray** about the problem to find the truth. Jesus is the truth; he said so in John 14:6.

- **Look** for alternatives.

- **Make** a decision or form an opinion based on what you've discovered. But be ready to think the topic through again if you learn about a new study or find new facts about the topic.

- **Choose** steps you can take to help solve the problem.

- **Be** patient and willing to keep working.

- **Write** to companies, agencies, or lawmakers to give your views on certain issues that affect our planet.

- **Pray** for God to guide your choices.

> *"I will guide you and teach you the way you should go. I will give you good advice and watch over you."*
>
> PSALM 32:8

Be Patient and Trust God

Real change takes faith in God's divine timing. Follow the example Jesus gave, in Luke 13:6–9, of a man who worked in a vineyard. The owner told the man to dig up and toss out a tree that didn't bear fruit. The man pleaded to take care of the tree one more year and said he would fertilize it and care for it. Be the person willing to keep trying to renew the earth. "'Sir,' the man replied, 'leave it alone for one more year. I'll dig around it and feed it. If it bears fruit next year, fine! If not, then cut it down.'" (Luke 13:8–9)

Kick Off an Eco-Club!

Start a Nature Girl club with friends! You could meet at church, school, park, or home. It's your club, so create it the way you want it with a mix of fun and focusing on caring for the earth. Pick a fun name, like The Green Scene Sisterhood.

1. **Recruit an adult** to be your advisor. This person would help you get permissions, check safety, listen to your plans, and give you advice.

2. **Snatch a place** to meet, and establish a regular time for meetings. It might be weekly, monthly, or every other Wednesday—whatever's most convenient for you and your crew. Be sure there's enough seating, good lighting, and tables to work on.

Nature Club

3. **Set some goals** for the group. Think about what you want to do and accomplish. Is the club to enjoy being outside more or to remind people to recycle? Do you want to plant trees and care for parks or make new crafts from old ones? Do you want to do a lot and maybe focus on one chapter of this book every month? Write your ideas down, discuss them, and then take a vote.

4. **Decide** if you want to charge dues and what the money would be used for. Once you have set some solid goals, think about what it costs to reach those goals and ways to raise the money. Decide if you will want to hold fundraisers that could help with projects like buying flowers to plant or helping to provide money for wells in other countries.

5. **Make plans.** You could plan what to do at the first few meetings, like sharing green news and ideas, or planning a big project such as planting a garden. You can decide if you'll want to take field trips to parks, garden centers, and animal shelters, or other places where you can learn more about going green and enjoying the outdoors. The trips should be related to the goals and projects you choose.

Expert Shout-out!

Word Keepers

A deputy assistant commissioner for the Bureau of Waste Prevention has this to say:

Hooray! Kid pledges really help. When kids ask their family to make a pledge to recycle, it works. Here's a simple one to make with your family and post near your trash:

My family pledges to actively participate in recycling by getting and using a curbside recycling bin or using a free drop-off site in our community.

Take Action!

Here are some recommended activities you and your club members could tackle:

- **Make a green pledge,** such as the one above, and ask everyone to have her family take the pledge and then spread out to the families in your school, church, or community.

- **Start a composting** pile at your school or church where people can snag compost soil for their gardens.

- **Work with a park** near your meeting place and find projects you can do to help the park and surrounding areas.

- **Kick off a litter campaign** to remind people to keep America beautiful. Form litter patrols to pick up litter weekly. Assign each group an area.

- **Conduct science experiments** related to the earth and cleaning up pollution. There are many in this book to try!

- **Host parties** or picnics at local parks. Have spa days where you invite friends or moms to come, enjoy, and learn about being green and beautiful. See Chapter 1 for spa party particulars!

- **Start a garden** to supply produce for a local shelter. A garden shop might even donate some plants or seeds for your project. Have club members pitch in and take turns caring for the garden.

✨ Real Girls ✨

The Club

"Shelly's here. Time for our meeting!" Girls looked forward to their weekly green club meeting called Beauty By God. Their adult leader, Shelly Ballestero, always mixed fun with faith and facts. Once club members heard about harmful ingredients in their fave products, like lip gloss, foundation, and shampoo, their reactions were, "Icky!" and "I don't want that on me!" The girls quickly let go of the diva desires for better choices and learned to make their own products, as well as treat their bodies better with healthy activities, and foods packed with good nutrients and vitamins.

Give 'em Lip!

Suppose after doing a little research, you find your fave lip gloss isn't exactly eco-friendly? Well, you have several choices. You could make the switch to a different lip gloss, or make your own (recipe on page 18). Or take it a step further: Write a letter to the company's staff to tell them why you stopped buying it and how much you want them to go green so you can put that lip gloss on with a smile.

You voice counts ... a lot! As a young person who has purchasing power, you absolutely have influence over many companies and their manufacturing choices. These companies know if you care, you'll influence what your friends buy and use. So if you take the time to write a letter or even send an e-mail, most company staffers will really listen up. How exciting that you can make a difference! So write letters to encourage companies to change for the better, and also write ones cheering companies that choose to be green. You can also write congressmen and other government officials to encourage them to change laws if needed.

To Make it Easy For You ...

Here's a sample letter: Just fill in the blanks, and write away to let your ideas and opinions be heard! For a standard snail-mail letter, put your name and address at the top center of the page, then fill in the company name and address below that to the left. In the body of the letter, avoid negative statements that criticize the company and instead state positively and clearly how you expect the company to be responsible for the environment.

_____
(Insert your name here)

_____
(Your address goes here)
(Name of company or government rep here)
(Company address inserted here)

To Whom It May Concern:

My name is _____ and I have been using your _____ for _____ years. It is my favorite brand of _____. I recently found out that you _____. This really concerns me because I feel that there are better choices that are kinder to our planet. I really like your products, but will only be able to resume using them if you are willing to _____.

Sincerely,

_____

Age _____

Great Cause? Hit Pause!

Don't be so wrapped up saving the world that you forget to breathe and enjoy all that's alive and wonderful around you. Capture beauty with your camera and pen. Sit and soak in nature and thank God for all he created. When you take walks, stop and praise God for the beauty and wonder surrounding you. It's good to take action toward positive change, but be sure to balance it with daily moments of stillness, meditation, appreciation, and prayer.

Going-Green Greeting Cards

Want to really get the attention of a politician or company official? Send your action letter on a handmade card that celebrates the beauty of the earth! Or send a nice card to a friend to share going-green tips. When making cards, use paper scraps from junk mail and even magazine pages. Remember that acid-free paper is more eco-friendly.

What you need:

Card bases or folded card stock (white, blue)
Glue or double-sided tape
Colored markers or pens
Brown and green paper scraps
Scissors
Black inkpad
Pencil with an eraser at one end
Envelopes for card size

Optional:

Ink in the color of leaves
Bird stickers

What to do:

1. The most popular size of cards (and cheapest to mail) is 4.25 by 5.5 inches. You can make these wide or tall. To make the card bases using the least paper, take an

8.5 by 11 sheet of paper and cut it in half. Then you can fold each half and have 2 card bases from 1 sheet.

2. If you want your card to look neater, then you might want to make your card front on a piece of paper the same size as the front of our card and then glue it on the card base. You can make the design directly on the base.

Card 1: "Tree-mendous" Card

This will be a tall card with a tree on the cover.

1. A good color for your card background would be blue. You can choose solid blue or you could choose a paper with a background design. The blue represents the sky.

2. To make your tree cut a rectangle about 2.5 by 3 inches from brown paper. This is the trunk so shape it a little bit by cutting slight curves along the two 3 inch sides. Next cut a variety of thin strips from your brown paper. Place the tree trunk and make a faint line across the top. Then pick up the trunk and use the line as a guide for where to add the branches coming out from the top and sides of the trunk. Once you have the branches glued down—glue the trunk of the tree down.

3. You have two choices for how to make your leaves. You can use green paper and tear it into small pieces and glue them on. Or use green ink and your thumb to make the leaves across the tree trunk. For a fall tree you can use yellow, orange, and red paper or ink.

4. Add a line of grass by cutting a piece of green paper that is 4.5 by 1 inch. Then cut fringe along the length of the paper to make grass. Glue this over the base of the tree.

5. If desired, add some clouds, sunshine, or birds in the sky by drawing or adding stickers.

6. Here's a sample message for writing inside your card:

Thanks for being a Tree-mendous friend of the earth!

Card 2: Accordion-folded Hands Card

A card cut in the shape of hands.

1. Using paper the color of your skin trace each of your hands. Then cut them out (or draw and cut small hands for a smaller card).
2. Write the phrase you want to use on a piece of paper and cut it so the paper is a long strip no wider than 1.5 inches high. Make sure you leave at least an inch of paper at the beginning and end of your phrase.
3. Fold the beginning edge of the written paper away from the writing and glue that section onto the inside of 1 hand.
4. Fold the paper back and forth ending with the paper folded away from the writing and glue the end of the paper onto the other hand.
5. When you bring the card together it should look like a hand and open up to reveal the message.
6. Sample message for the hand cards:

Gotta hand it to ya! You really reach out to care for the earth!

Card 3: Animal Tracks Card

Choose a tall or long card for this one.

1. Use a light brown as your background to be the ground the animal tracks are left on.
2. Use black ink and your fingerprints as well as a pencil point to make tracks.
3. For bird tracks (three-toed prints of birds) use a sharp pencil (or the end of a mechanical pencil with the lead inside) and press it onto a black inkpad. Then put your pencil down at a point and draw a short line from the point straight out that is about half an inch long. Add

new ink to your pencil and then put it down at the point you started last time. This time draw the line out at a slight diagonal line. Make a third line diagonal from the point on the opposite side of the straight line to finish off the track. Make a line of these tracks across the card.

4. To make a small mammal's tracks, start by putting your index finger into the ink and making an oval dot on the page. Ink you finger once again, this time setting your finger down at a slight angle, making it almost like a heart shape for the base of the footprint. Then using a pointed pencil dip it into the ink and put it down slightly in front of the base of the footprint you have made—drag it slightly to make it look like the front claw of the print. Make three to five of these claws off the base to make the complete print. Make prints across the card.

5. Sample message for the animal track cards:

Paws and enjoy nature!

Picture Perfect

Photojournalism is a great way to share your passion for going green. You can make albums or scrapbooks, use pictures on cards, or print and hang some in your  room. Take photos whenever you're doing something green. Snap pics of waterways, critters, healthy foods, or plants.

Here are a few tips for taking good shots:

- It helps to have a zoom feature telescopic lens and sports setting to capture flying birds and scampering animals. Zoom in for close up without moving and scaring creatures.

- A sports setting (for cameras with a fast shutter speed) takes three to four photos in a row to photograph motion.

- The higher the number setting of film or camera setting the faster the camera can snap photos. Many cameras have a shutter speed dial.

- Print several small individual photos from animals in motion to make a flipbook. Layer the pictures in order and then use a finger to flip through the photos and see the motion.

I like to take pictures of the sunset. My favorite picture I took was at my aunts house and I got a great picture of the sun peeking over the mountain as it set!

— CHLOE, AGE 11, MARYLAND

Make an Eco-Scrapbook

Use photos of nature, clipart, and magazine pictures to make creative scrapbook pages:

What you need:
Photos
Scrapbook paper
Acid free adhesive

What to do:
1. Pick your photos first and choose things that will look good with your pictures.
2. Play with where to place pictures before gluing anything.
3. Use the rule of thirds. Think of your paper as divided into an invisible tic-tac-toe board. Anything you place

along the lines will be a place your eyes are more naturally drawn to—so place titles and the eyes of the person in your main picture along a line of the board.

4. Use layers. Layer various papers to help make interesting backgrounds. You can also use paints or mists to make additional layers.

5. Try making a simple misted background. Collect items with interesting shapes and place them on a solid colored paper. Take a mist (available at craft stores) and spray it across the paper. Remove the objects. You'll see negative space of the objects as a background on the paper. Layer photos over the design to make a great page.

6. You can also make a background paper by using items from nature as stamps. Dip a leaf, sticks, or another object in paint or ink and then place it down on the paper. When you pick it up you will have left the shape to use as a layer on your paper. You can stamp the same object a few times or different ones each time to make backgrounds.

Quiz

Are You Walking On the Green Side?

Going green can be a quite satisfying (and sometimes challenging) journey. Take this quiz to gauge how far along you are on the path to going green.

1. To visit a friend ...
   a. Mom drives me
   b. I get dropped off when mom is going that way
   c. I bike or walk

2. In the past month, I ...
   a. Enjoyed playing or walking in a park
   b. Cleaned up part of my yard
   c. Took part in a cleanup effort in my community
   d. Did at least two of the above.

3. When I leave a room, I ...
   a. Make sure I look cute and maybe wear something green
   b. At least turn off the lights
   c. Check and turn off any electronics

4. I conserve water by ...
   a. Brushing my teeth less
   b. Taking shorter showers
   c. Checking for drips and leaks

5. I help air quality by ...
   a. Keeping air fresheners
   b. Carpooling more
   c. Walking or riding my bike

6. When it comes to healthful food choices ...
   a. Well, I like my snacks and junk food
   b. I eat my vegetables like Mom says
   c. I eat very little junk food and lots of local produce

7. I care for local streams, lakes, or oceans by ...
   a. Swimming and boating in them
   b. Not washing the family car in the driveway
   c. Staying out of the water
   d. Taking pictures of the waterways

8. Wind barriers prevent soil erosion. They can be ...
   a. Shrubs planted to block wind
   b. Straw, hay, old cornstalks, or other plant residue spread over the ground
   c. a and b
   d. Scarecrows

9. Using eco-friendly soap ...
   a. Both b and c
   b. Allows water to flow further and wet more ground
   c. Loosens soil like the soap loosens dirt from dishes
   d. Gives plants a bubble bath

10. Building a bird house helps ...

   a. Birds hide from animals that want to kill them
   b. Provide shelter to feathered friends from rain, wind, and cold
   c. Birds live in luxury accommodations
   d. a and b

11. I'm glam and green because I ...
   a. Care for my skin and the earth
   b. Wash my hair with eco-friendly shampoo
   c. Rock my self-confidence and do something green daily
   d. Do all the above

12. I recycled or reused something ...
   a. Today
   b. This week
   c. Soon

13. As I flip through this book, I ...
    a. Glance at facts and check out the quizzes
    b. Enjoy the crafts and some of the activities
    c. Learn a lot and am trying to do many of the activities that help the earth

Scoring:

#1-6: 1 point for every a, 2 points for every b, and 3 points for every c answer

#7: 1 point for a or d, 3 points for b, and 0 for c

#8: 1 point for a or b, 3 points for c, and 0 for d

#9: 3 points for a, 2 points for b or c, and 0 for d

#10: 2 points for a or c, 0 for b, and 3 points for d

#11: 1 point for a of b, 2 points for c, and 4 points for d

#12: 3 points for a, 2 points for b, and o for c

#13: 1 point for a or b, 3 points for c

0-10 Points: Slippery Slope

Um ... get off the couch, kick off your slippers, pull on your hiking boots, go outdoors, and start the green journey. Since you seem to have some trepidation, you can start in small doses. For now, vow to apply ideas in this book to do something green each week.

11-20 points: Steppin' Out

You've veered out of the mall long enough to start your green journey in life. Be eco-conscious, and do a little more each week. Check out parks, recycle, and try to conserve more resources. Journal about what you do, and discover as you continue on your green walk in life.

21-30 points: Trekking Along

You're happily following along on the green path, helping to make the world better while enjoying nature. There's still more you can do, so check back through some of the ideas and activities in the book and take a stab at a few more.

31-40 points: Walking Like Wild!

Snaps! You have full-on embraced being green and caring for the world God made. Share your love of nature with friends ... and remember to slow down, earth angel. Be sure to take time to relax and enjoy the beauty around you.

Eco-Careers

Environmental Activism

- **Environmental Lawyer**

  "I handle permits and help with legal issues about land and the environment."

- **Science Teacher**

  "I teach students about various sciences like physics, chemistry, and earth science."

- **Urban and Regional Planner**

  "I develop plans for using land in towns, cities, and counties."

- **Construction Worker**

  "I build homes and try to make them earth friendly. I also try to use the latest methods to save energy."

Resources

Books

Carroll, Michael, and Caroline Carroll. *I Love God's Green Earth: Devotions for Kids Who Want to Take Care of God's Creation.* Carol Stream, IL: Tyndale Kids, 2010.

Amsel, Sheri. *365 Ways to Live Green for Kids: Saving the Environment at Home, School, or at Play—Every Day!* Avon, MA: Adams Media, 2009.

Ballestero, Shelly. *Beauty By God: Inside Out Secrets for Every Woman.* Ventura, CA: Regal, 2009.

Javna, John. *The New 50 Simple Things Kids Can Do to Save the Earth.* Kansas City, MO: The Earthworks Group/Andrews McMeel, 2009.

MacEachern, Diane. *Big Green Purse: Use Your Spending Power to Create a Cleaner, Greener World.* New York: Penguin Group, 2008.

Provey, Joe, and Owen Lockwood. *The Little Green Book: 365 Ways to Love the Planet.* Upper Saddle River, NJ: Creative Homeowner, 2008.

Sleeth, Emma. *It's Easy Being Green: One Student's Guide to Serving God and Saving the Planet.* Grand Rapids, MI: Zondervan, 2008.

Online Sources

Secondary Materials and Recycled Textiles Association, http://www.smart.org

US Department of Agriculture. USDA. *Organic Certification.* 2011. Print. http://www.usda.gov/wps/portal/usda/usdahome?navid =ORGANIC_CERTIFICATIO&parentnav=AGRICULTURE &navtype=RT.

US National Park Service, http://www.nps.gov/

Experts

Ballestero, Shelly (http://www.shellyballestero.com): a licensed esthetician, makeup artist, a former beauty columnist, and author of a book on beauty.

Chapman, Travis: a nuclear engineer and part of the technical staff of the Defense Nuclear Facilities Safety Board (DNFSB). He also serves in the Navy Reserves.

Dakin, Karin (http://www.dakindairyfarms.com): the co-owner of Dakin Farms in Myakka City, Florida. She oversees the entire farming operation.

Hartigan, Jerome: a marine engineer consultant and lead engineer in refueling nuclear power plants.

Hernandez, Anthony: a soil conservation technician with the National Resources Conservation Service (NRCS) with a degree in environmental studies.

King, Jackie: Executive Director of Secondary Materials And Recycled Textiles (SMART) Association.

Kieffer, Joy: a landscape artist.

Noon, Marita: an author, speaker, and executive director of two non-profit organizations—Energy Makes America Great and Citizen's Alliance for Responsible Energy.

Pierce, Martha: a master naturalist, is a camp director for environmentally conscientious Riverside Retreat Center.

Sanchez, Olga: holds a college degree in environmental studies and is the lab manager at the Southeastern Environmental Research Center at Florida International University.

Steer, Dr. Andrew: a climate control specialist and president of World Resources International.

Stewart, Lori: a certified plant professional and landscape designer.

Strickland, Jennifer (www.jenniferstrickland.net): an author, speaker, and former international model.

Weinstein, Sarah: the deputy assistant commissioner for the Bureau of Waste Prevention in the Massachusetts Department of Environmental Protection, has a degree is in city planning and studied environmental planning.

Whiting, Dr. James: electrical and aerospace engineer.

Shopping Guide

www.fromnaturewithlove.com

We want to hear from you. Please send your comments about this book to us in care of zreview@zondervan.com. Thank you.